Books by Mark Cheverton

The Gameknight999 Series
Invasion of the Overworld
Battle for the Nether
Confronting the Dragon

The Mystery of Herobrine Series: A Gameknight999 Adventure
Trouble in Zombie-town
The Jungle Temple Oracle
Last Stand on the Ocean Shore

Herobrine Reborn Series: A Gameknight999 Adventure
Saving Crafter
The Destruction of the Overworld
Gameknight999 vs. Herobrine

Herobrine's Revenge Series: A Gameknight999 Adventure
The Phantom Virus
Overworld in Flames
System Overload

The Birth of Herobrine: A Gameknight999 Adventure
The Great Zombie Invasion
Attack of the Shadow-Crafters
Herobrine's War

The Mystery of Entity303: A Gameknight999 Adventure
Terrors of the Forest (Coming Soon!)
Monsters in the Mist (Coming Soon!)
Mission to the Moon (Coming Soon!)

The Gameknight999 Box Set
The Gameknight999 vs. Herobrine Box Set

The Algae Voices of Azule Series
Algae Voices of Azule
Finding Home
Finding the Lost

AN UNOFFICIAL NOVEL

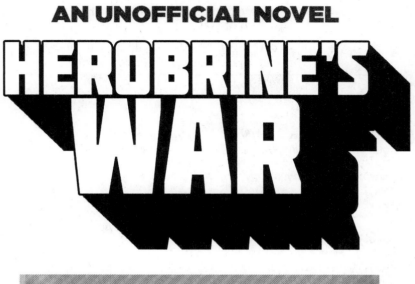

HEROBRINE'S WAR

THE BIRTH OF HEROBRINE
BOOK THREE
<<< A GAMEKNIGHT999 ADVENTURE >>>

AN UNOFFICIAL MINECRAFTER'S ADVENTURE

MARK CHEVERTON

SKY PONY PRESS
NEW YORK

Sky Pony Press books may be purchased in bulk at special discounts for sales promotion, corporate gifts, fund-raising, or educational purposes. Special editions can also be created to specifications. For details, contact the Special Sales Department, Sky Pony Press, 307 West 36th Street, 11th Floor, New York, NY 10018 or info@skyhorsepublishing.com.

Sky Pony® is a registered trademark of Skyhorse Publishing, Inc.®, a Delaware corporation.

Visit our website at www.skyponypress.com.

10 9 8 7 6 5 4 3 2 1

Library of Congress Cataloging-in-Publication Data is available on file.

Cover design by Owen Corrigan
Cover artwork by Thomas Frick
Technical consultant: Gameknight999

Print ISBN: 978-1-5107-0996-6
Ebook ISBN: 978-1-5107-1001-6

Printed in Canada

ACKNOWLEDGMENTS

As always, I'd like to give a big thank you to my family. Without their help and support, I'd never be able to maintain this pace of a book every other month. I'd also like to thank my editor, Cory Allyn. Without his sharp eye for mixed metaphors and repeated phrases, none of these books would sparkle as they do. To my agent, Holly Root, the best agent in the business, I thank you for your continual faith in me, and enthusiasm about these projects.

Of course, I want to thank all of you, the readers. It is your excitement about my stories and my characters that gets me up at 6:00 a.m. to write and keeps me writing through the late night and weekends.

To all of the teachers that are using my books to get kids excited about reading, I am incredibly grateful. Your stories about your students getting excited about reading are heartwarming to hear. On my website, www.markcheverton, I've posted some resources that might help to inspire even *more* kids to read and write. Thank you for everything you do. Teaching kids to love learning is an important and, at times, difficult job. So, thank you for your hard work and dedication; you're making a difference in the lives of many.

NOTE FROM THE AUTHOR

I had a lot of fun writing this trilogy, and sending Gameknight999 back in time. It was exciting to explore what Crafter's ancestors were like. Hopefully, I'll see some new stories sent to my website, www.markcheverton.com, from my readers about some of these new characters. Maybe there will even be a few stories about the budding romance that starts near the end of this book? That would be cool.

It is really awesome to be receiving stories from all of you. I know a few of you have actually self-published your stories, like Elijah P, Danny O, Ryan T, and Elijah S. I think that's super cool. If you're thinking about writing, but need a little bit of help to get your story started, then go to my website and click on the "For Teachers" tab. You'll find many video tutorials, as well as writing guides and information about writing. In these materials, I describe the process of writing a short story, "Battle with the Wither King." You can see how I sat down to create an outline, as well as the final finished story. Show this page to your teachers; maybe you can use these videos and work on writing your own stories in your classes at school. I hope you find the videos and information helpful; I'll be adding more in the future.

In the Minecraft Seeds section at the end of this book, you might notice that two of them are missing: the waterfall and Olympus Mons. I'll be building those in Minecraft so you can see what I was imagining when I wrote the book. Go to www.gameknight999.com to find more information about the Gameknight999 Minecraft Network. If you log in (with your parent's permission!) and go to the survival server, type the command */warp bookwarps*. You'll see the bookwarps for all of my books there. Come onto the server and meet others that read my books. The IP address is *mc.gameknight999.com*. Maybe you'll see my son, Gameknight999, and me, Monkeypants_271.

While on gameknight999.com, look around and you'll find some additional free short stories I've been writing, as well as some images you can download. I'll be adding more short stories through the year, so keep checking. Download them, send them to your friends, even send them to your teacher! I hope you enjoy.

Keep reading, and watch out for creepers.
Mark

Trying to do everything by yourself, like Sisyphus pushing that rock up the hill by himself, is difficult, pointless, and makes those around you think you don't trust them. Open yourself to the help of friends and Sisyphus's rock will make it all the way to the top of the hill and stay there, if supported by friends.

CHAPTER 1

MALACODA

The world around him wanted to be enslaved; it just didn't know it yet. Herobrine would soon teach all the creatures of Minecraft that he was their master. But first he had to control his overwhelming rage.

"How could that pathetic blacksmith and those villagers defeat us again?!" the evil virus screamed in frustration.

He glanced around at the surviving monsters that stood nearby. The zombies and skeletons looked terrified, fearing Herobrine would unleash his wrath upon them. They were wise to keep their distance, for he was considering doing exactly that. But even though it might give him momentary pleasure, deep down, he knew destroying a few dozen zombies would not help him in the long run.

Nearby, the king of the Endermen, Erebus, stood tall and confident, his dark-red skin standing out in bright contrast to the skeletons and zombies that shuffled around him. The creature's red eyes glowed bright with anger. When Herobrine had created Erebus, he'd poured all his malice and vile hatred for the villages into the creature's soul, and now, he, too, was furious that they had been defeated.

A clicking sound floated out of the desert and echoed off the four steep mountains surrounding them. The peaks were called Dragon's Teeth, and were currently Herobrine's base. Herobrine had formed his massive monster army here, between these four spires, just before moving against that blacksmith, Smithy, and his rabble of villager NPCs (non-playable characters). They had outnumbered the enemy five-to-one, if not more, and yet they still lost.

"That Smithy always has some trick up his sleeve," Herobrine growled.

Just then, the clicking sound grew louder, as if a million crickets were arriving. But instead, a large group of spiders emerged out of the nearby forest, led by the spider queen, Shaikulud. The eight bright purple eyes on her large, fuzzy black head glowed with the same rage felt by Herobrine and Erebus. She, too, was furious at their loss; hundreds of her spiders had been destroyed during the battle.

"We musssst exact our revenge on the villag-erssss," the spider queen hissed. "That old hag, the Oracle, desssstroyed hundredsssss of my ssssspi-derssss. Sssshe musssst be eliminated."

"You will get your revenge, Shaikulud," Herobrine growled. "That I promise."

"Without the creepers, getting past the defenses of the villagers proves difficult," Erebus pointed out.

"The creepers!" Herobrine hissed, his rage barely held in check. "The king of the creepers,

Oxus, has chosen to run away and hide rather than sacrifice his followers in my war. His treachery and cowardice caused this defeat." The evil artificially-intelligent virus paced back and forth, his eyes glowing brighter. "Some day I will find that cowardly creeper and teach him what happens to those who defy Herobrine. But, for now, we must concentrate on Smithy and his pathetic villagers."

"We need a way to get past their walls," Erebus said in a high-pitched, screechy voice. "Without the creepers, more frontal assaults will only prove suicidal. We cannot win that way."

Herobrine closed his eyes and teleported right next to the king of the Endermen. He glared up at the tall, lanky creature.

"We will win this war how ever I *say* we will win," Herobrine snarled, his eyes growing dangerously bright as his temper grew hot. "If I say the monsters must make a suicidal charge against the villagers' walls, then that is what they will do."

"Yes, my Maker," Erebus replied, lowering his head to show deference to his leader. "But . . . if there were a way to fire over their walls from high in the air, it would help. Their walls and defenses. . . ."

"Be silent!" Herobrine snapped.

An idea suddenly materialized in his evil mind.

Glancing up at the sky, he noticed pristine white ghasts playing innocently amongst the rectangular clouds, their cube-like bodies and long tentacles drifting with the misty shapes as if the floating giants had no cares.

Turning, Herobrine stared at the lone blaze who had survived the last battle. The creature of smoke and flame was floating above the lava flow that spilled down one of the Dragon's Teeth, its glowing blaze rods spinning quickly around its central, life-giving flame. Slowly, the blaze lowered itself into the molten stone and drank in the heat, rejuvenating its HP (health points).

"You, blaze: follow me," Herobrine ordered.

The creature turned its orange, glowing head, its two ink-black eyes staring back at Herobrine, terrified.

Before it could answer, Herobrine teleported to the tallest of the Dragon's Teeth. The sheer mountain had patches of snow covering the few horizontal surfaces that made up its sloping surfaces. At the top, the dark shadow-crafter was up so high that he was above the clouds, and could look down upon the ghasts as they played amongst themselves like innocent children. One of the huge, boxy creatures drifted nearby. With lightning speed, Herobrine reached out and grabbed one of its tentacles, then drew it near. The creature didn't squirm or struggle or try to get away. It lacked the ability to even consider a negative or violent thought; they were completely innocent in both mind and deed. So the ghast allowed itself to be drawn to the rocky peak.

Pulling his iron sword from his inventory, Herobrine stuck the white monster. The floating beast looked down at his attacker with a confused expression on its square, baby-like face. He hit the ghast again. This time, it gave off a cat-like cry as the creature's eyes darted to the left and right, confused and scared. With one last hit, the creature slowly fell, its HP no longer able to hold it aloft.

Pulling the slowly deflating gasbag toward him, Herobrine settled it on the surface of the jagged peak. He positioned the wounded ghast carefully on the peak so it would fall. As he adjusted the terrified creature, a mechanical wheezing sound began to fill the air, the acrid smell of ash and soot floating toward him on the constant east-to-west breeze. The blaze had finally made it to the top of the Dragon's Tooth. Herobrine gestured for it to come closer, and the blaze drifted so it was directly over the suffering ghast.

The virus's sword was a blur as it flashed across the blaze's body, rending the HP from the internal flame. The Maker hit it again and again, bringing the fiery creature to the brink of death. It, too, eventually collapsed onto the rocky spire, atop the ghast.

Reaching out with his viral crafting abilities, Herobrine drew the code-modifying powers into his body. A pale-yellow glow slowly covered his hands, then grew brighter as it spread up his arms like an insipid disease. Kneeling at the side of the two creatures, Herobrine drew the two beings together and began to sculpt, his powers modifying the computer code that defined their shapes. Pushing one into the other, the monsters started to merge. The blaze disappeared as the larger body of the ghast began to inflate with a fiery core. Concentrating on his hatred for the villagers, Herobrine filled the new creature with a sense of loathing for everything good and honest and kind. He made his new creation a thing overflowing with violence and malice. It would be one of his most magnificent creations, just like the rest of his monster kings and queens, for the great Herobrine could do no less. And with these thoughts, his arrogant confidence filled the few empty spaces left within the monster.

Finally, with the ghast fully inflated, he was finished.

"Arise, my child," Herobrine said, his eyes glowing bright with evil delight. "Arise and take your place as the king of the ghasts. I name you Malacoda, and you will now be my instrument of destruction."

The ghast rose into the air and looked down at Herobrine, his eyes blood-red and glowing with anger and rage for the NPCs of the Overworld.

"Where are my minions?" Malacoda asked.

His voice sounded almost baby-like, with a hint of feline to it. Herobrine smiled. It made the creature seem even more terrifying.

"You're right. You have no troops . . . yet."

Closing his eyes, the Maker reached out into the fabric of Minecraft. Drawing on the lines of code that made up Malacoda, he projected them to the other ghasts nearby and focused his mind's eye on his targets. Suddenly, there was a clap of thunder as bolts of pale-yellow lightning sprung from Herobrine's fingertips. The shafts of light struck the nearby monsters, blasting them with the Maker's code-altering viral poison. Instantly, the ghasts cried out in pain and fear as confused expressions filled their innocent faces. But after the lightning strike, they no longer looked so innocent. There was something sinister about the creatures now, even though their pristine white bodies and baby-like faces remained the same.

"Come forth and meet your ruler," Herobrine shouted, his voice booming through the sky.

They drew near, each one looking at the ground, searching for a target to attack. Slowly, the white cubes floated over to Herobrine and Malacoda and bowed, showing respect for their king, as well as their Maker.

Herobrine surveyed his new monsters. There were thirteen of them, counting Malacoda. It was not many, but it was a start.

"I have infused each of you with the powers of the blazes," Herobrine explained as he sat down on a snow-covered block of gravel. Making the ghasts had taken a lot out of him. He worried how he was going to make a vast army of the creatures without depleting his own XP (experience points). "All of you now have a new ability." He turned to face the king of the ghasts. "Malacoda, do you see that cow down there on the ground?"

The big ghast turned his glowing red eyes to the ground, then nodded.

"Go down there and destroy it," Herobrine commanded.

The ghast looked confused, but floated toward the innocent cow anyway. As he neared, Herobrine called out.

"Think of that cow as a villager, your enemy," the Maker shouted. "Destroy the villager."

A ball of fire began to grow amidst the creature's tentacles, casting a warm, orange glow on its writhing appendages. The ball grew bigger and bigger.

"NOW . . . ATTACK!" Herobrine screamed.

Malacoda somehow sucked the flaming sphere up into its body, then spit the ball of death at the unsuspecting bovine. It smashed into the black-and-white animal, the flames enveloping the creature and burning away its HP until it disappeared with a *pop*.

"Ha ha!" Herobrine laughed. "This is your new ability. You will attack the villagers from the air, and their walls will be unable to protect them. As your numbers grow, we will soon be rid of the disease that infects these servers . . . the villagers!"

Erebus began to chuckle as the spider queen clicked her mandibles together, her eyes glowing bright.

"We will rule the land *and* rule the air!" Herobrine screamed from atop the Dragon's Tooth. "Nothing will stop us, not even that cowardly blacksmith, Smithy."

Herobrine's eyes flared bright with evil thoughts as he imagined what he was going to do to his enemy, Smithy of the Two-swords.

CHAPTER 2
RETURNING HOME

The army trudged across the rolling sand dunes in the Great Northern Desert. To their left, a line of tall mountains stretched out both ahead and behind them as far as the eye could see. Gameknight999 knew they had travelled a long way from the desert village they'd left behind.

"You think Carver and the other villagers were glad to see us leave?" Fencer asked. "After all, we did bring a war with us to their doorstep."

Gameknight looked at the NPC. He wore a light-brown smock with a white stripe running down the middle, the clothing only visible around his neck and near his feet; his iron armor hid all the rest. He was a large villager, bigger than most, with muscular arms and strong broad shoulders. Salt-and-pepper black hair ringed the sides of his square head, but the top was completely bald. In the harsh desert sun, Fencer was slowly getting sunburned, and would need to put on his iron helmet soon. Most of the villagers had taken off their helmets; they were uncomfortable to wear in the hot sun.

But Gameknight kept his metal cap on his boxy head.

It was part of his disguise. He'd been posing as the great leader Smithy, the blacksmith, and the helmet hid his small nose and user-like features from the other villagers. As far as he knew, his real identity still remained hidden from them.

"We didn't bring war with us—Herobrine did," Gameknight said. "They were just unfortunate enough to be in its path, just like all the other villages and NPCs he's attacked."

"Yeah, I know, but they're probably still glad we're gone," Fencer added. "Now they can get back to their regular lives."

"None of us are going to get back to our regular lives until Herobrine is stopped, for good," Gameknight said. "But I'm glad we destroyed his army back there in the desert. I think it'll be a while before the monsters are ready to attack again. The ones that survived that battle are probably scattered all across the Overworld. But you can be certain Herobrine is planning some new and evil scheme, even as we speak."

"You sound a little paranoid," a young NPC said as a small pig trotted up to walk along at their side.

"Oink," the pig said.

"Now Wilbur, don't you go taking Weaver's side in this," Gameknight said with a smile.

"I can't help it if Wilbur is a smart pig," Weaver added.

"Oink, oink."

Gameknight smiled at Weaver. The boy's dark-brown hair was matted against his forehead, the tangles falling down around his shoulders. Those locks always seemed to be in need of a comb, though combs didn't exist in Minecraft. Gameknight still marveled at the adolescent's bright blue eyes. It was as if they were glowing from within, lit by his exuberant and positive personality. He was the ancestor of one of Gameknight's friends in the present day; Weaver was Crafter's great uncle.

Somehow, for reasons still unknown, Gameknight had been transported into Minecraft's past when he used his father's invention, the Digitizer, to travel into the game. He wasn't just a user, but something more (or less, depending on how you looked at it); he was the User-that-is-not-a-user, the protector of Minecraft.

It wasn't clear when the Digitizer would bring him back into the physical world, but until it did, Gameknight was going to do whatever was necessary to protect the villagers he met, to prevent his friends' ancestors from being harmed. If someone like Weaver, his friend's great uncle, was killed, then what might happen to his friend in the future? Gameknight999 didn't know, and was determined not to find out.

Suddenly, a cat-like yowl filled the air, followed by what sounded like a baby's cry. Gameknight instantly drew his diamond sword and glanced skyward.

"It's just a ghast," Fencer said. "You don't need to worry about them. All they do is play around up in the clouds . . . they're completely harmless."

"So you say, but I don't trust them," Gameknight replied.

He saw a single cloud moving slowly across the sky, a group of nine tentacles hanging just below the misty rectangle.

In Gameknight's time, ghasts were deadly creatures that only lived in the Nether. He'd fought them many times, and had seen the floating monsters destroy countless NPCs. But, for some reason, in Minecraft's distant past, ghasts where harmless, like innocent children the villagers basically ignored.

An angry cry filled the air again. Gameknight drew his iron sword, now holding two blades. It was how he'd earned his moniker, Smithy of the Two-swords. Glancing to the east, he saw one of the floating white cubes slowly descend from a cloud, the nine tentacles of the ghast squirming and writhing like a nest of vipers.

"Everyone, get ready!" Gameknight shouted.

The villagers laughed.

He ignored them and moved toward the monster. There was something different about the creature. It had a sinister and evil look to its eyes, though he couldn't quite pinpoint what had changed. It lacked the scars on its face that ghasts possessed in Gameknight's time, and it didn't have the infamous tear-shaped markings under its large eyes either. But there was still something about this monster that looked wrong . . . and evil.

Suddenly, its eyes changed from narrow, dark slits to large circles, blood-red pupils at their center. The creature had an evil look to it, as if you were staring into the eyes of one of the monster kings, or maybe Herobrine himself. Its mouth opened wide and spat a large fireball directly at Gameknight. He was terrified. The dark-brown leather armor that he wore, part of the disguise to make him look like Smithy, would do little to protect him against this blazing sphere of death.

The fireball shot straight at Gameknight999. Timing it carefully, he swung his diamond sword at the fiery ball just before it struck. His blade deflected it safely away.

Putting away his swords, he drew his bow and began firing back at the creature, yelling as loud as he could.

"We're being attacked!"

The other villagers now took notice, many of them staring at the ghast in disbelief, unable to comprehend how or why it had attacked.

"Don't stand still," Gameknight shouted as he ran erratically across the sands, making himself as difficult to hit as possible. "Keep moving at all times."

The ghast fired again. The burning sphere wasn't aimed at him this time, and the distraction gave Gameknight time to stop for an instant and aim. He fired three quick arrows at the monster, but as the missiles sped towards it, the creature rose. As a result, the arrows flew under its wriggling tentacles and missed their target.

Another fireball streaked down towards the ground and hit one of the villagers. Instantly, he was engulfed in flames. But before the NPC could utter a sound, Weaver was there with a bucket of water, quenching the terrible fire. A builder and a baker came to the wounded villager's aid, and caught him as he slumped to the ground, his HP dangerously low.

"Shoot at the ghast!" Gameknight yelled as he fired three more shots.

The first two of his arrows struck the monster, but the third missed; it was still alive. The monster's eyes grew large again as it prepared for another attack. But before it could launch a flaming ball of death, a string of arrows flew up from the ground and hit the monster, taking the last of its HP. It disappeared with a *pop*, dropping three glowing balls of XP. But it left behind no ghast tears, which Gameknight would have expected in the present-day Minecraft.

Turning, the User-that-is-not-a-user found Weaver standing nearby, his bow out and another arrow notched.

"Nice shooting, Weaver," Fencer said. "The rest of us were a little shocked. We've never seen a ghast do that before."

"Don't talk; look around and see if there are more of those monsters," Gameknight said as he scanned the sky.

The blue sky shone down upon him from all directions. There were no floating white cubes drifting towards them, nor were there any tentacles visible below the clouds. The attack had just been from a single ghast; no armies of airborne monsters were about to descend down upon them, at least not yet.

But the thought they might eventually attack again made Gameknight shudder.

He moved to the three glowing balls of XP that floated nearby and allowed them to flow into his body. He then turned to face the villagers.

"You see? I told you ghasts were evil," Gameknight said.

"That has never happened before," Fencer said. "We didn't even know they could throw fireballs."

"Herobrine," Gameknight said, spitting the name out as if it were venom on his tongue. "He must have done something to them, altered the ghasts to make them evil."

"That can't be good," Fencer said.

The User-that-is-not-a-user shook his head in agreement.

"We need to get to the villages and warn them," Gameknight said. "I know how to fight them, so we must spread the word. But first, we have to warn Carver's village back in the desert. They're closest to Herobrine's stronghold at Dragon's Teeth, and will likely be the first to feel the sting of that evil virus's latest scheme."

"I'll do it," one villager said. "I can go warn them."

By the look of his clothing, a dark-blue smock with a white stripe running down the center, the User-that-is-not-a-user guessed he was a fisherman.

"Fisher is the fastest person from our village," Fencer explained. "He'll get through to them."

"Okay," Gameknight said, then moved to the NPC's side. "Fisher, don't take any chances. If you see a ghast, run for cover. Don't try to hit the fireballs away like I just did; it's very difficult to do and takes a lot of practice. Just run and hide . . . you got it?"

The villager nodded his head.

"Okay, go!"

The NPC took off sprinting across the desert as the rest of them moved to the opening of Two-sword Pass; it was the only way through the mountain range. They followed the winding, narrow passage in silence, their faces creased with sadness. The only sound filling the air was that of armored plates slapping against thighs and shoulders as the army walked.

Every one of them could remember the battle that had happened here not too long ago. The zombie king, Vo-Lok, had led Herobrine's forces against them. But even though the villagers had prevailed, destroying the king of the zombies and his army, the cost in NPC lives had been severe.

Gameknight remembered the moment when the real Smithy had given him his armor and black-smith's hammer, just before he died. Only Fencer and Gameknight had witnessed the passing of the great leader, and only those two knew the truth: Gameknight999 was posing as their leader, Smithy.

Now, it felt as if Gameknight were to come clean and tell the truth, the villagers might turn on him, and maybe even shun him from their community. He couldn't bear that rejection. Instead, he and Fencer maintained the lie, convincing themselves that it was the only way the NPCs would have a leader; without Smithy of the Two-swords, the army would likely be defeated by Herobrine.

That ghast back there had frightened a lot of vil-lagers, and they looked to their blacksmith to keep them safe. But Gameknight knew the lone ghast had to be some kind of warning. Something about it seemed wrong. Gameknight had no proof, but he'd bet everything he had that Herobrine had some-thing bigger in mind than infecting a single ghast. The evil virus always had enormous, destructive schemes, and if Herobrine could infect one mon-ster with his vile hatred, then he could likely infect many.

Gameknight999 glanced at the Oracle and gave her a worried look. She had been sent into Minecraft to stop Herobrine; he was a virus, and she was the anti-virus. But so far, they'd only managed to keep him in check, and had made little progress in destroying him. If he added an army of ghasts to his arsenal of monsters, then the NPCs were in serious trouble.

CHAPTER 3

DESPERATE RUN

Fisher ran to the east, away from the army. Glancing over his shoulder, he watched the villagers, his friends, as they disappeared into Two-sword Pass. He'd been there when the narrow passage through the mountain range had been named. Smithy, their leader, had somehow picked up two swords in battle, one of them his own, and the other belonging to that stranger from another land, Gameknight999, who everyone said had died in the fighting.

Fisher remembered: he had been up on an archer tower when he heard Smithy's battle cry. He'd looked down, and saw his leader heroically holding up two swords, with Gameknight's armor lying on the ground next to him. That had been the moment when everything changed. The sight of Smithy with the two swords had been so inspiring, everyone fought harder than they ever had before, and refused to back down.

Smithy of the Two-swords had charged out to confront all of the monsters by himself. But the other villages chose to run out with him and fight at his side, including Fisher. They had pushed the monsters deep into the desert, then finally destroyed them. Their victory had been incredible, and Fisher would never forget that moment when their blacksmith had stepped up and become a true hero.

But now, running through the desert, alone, Fisher didn't feel so brave. Every time a dried bush rustled, he jumped. Every time he ran up a sand dune and saw a prickly green cactus, he jumped. Every time he saw anything, like a cloud in the sky, he was terrified. It had seemed like a good idea to volunteer for this mission, to warn Carver's desert village that danger was likely heading their way, but now it didn't seem like a very smart move.

Glancing at the sky, he saw some clouds moving in from the east, floating ominously over the desert in his direction. Something about those clouds caused an icy shiver to go down his spine.

"I'm just imagining things," he said aloud to the empty desert. "Clouds can't harm me."

Then, a faint feline cry slowly drifted to him on the wind. Fisher couldn't tell where exactly it was coming from, or if it was just his mind playing tricks, his fear getting the better of him. Gritting his teeth, he continued to run across the sandy dunes, intent on reaching the desert village as quickly as possible, but also knowing he was still very far away.

Another soft, cat-like yowl startled him, and this time it was unmistakably coming from over-head, followed with what sounded like a baby's cry. Glancing up to the sky, Fisher saw nine tentacles slowly drop through the cloud above him, a large, square body attached to the writhing, snake-like things.

"Ghast!" he hissed.

Quickly, he pulled out a shovel and began to work. It was easy digging through the sand, and he soon had a hole that stretched down three blocks. He placed a cube of sandstone over his head, sealing himself inside. Holding out a torch, he saw areas in front of him that were made of sandstone, and started to dig those up, while still keeping one block in place so the sand overhead wouldn't crash down upon him.

Fisher stuck the torch in the ground as he worked. It cast a wide circle of flickering light, filling in the shadows and driving back the imaginary monsters his scared mind was creating. Moving up to the topmost block, he pressed his ear against it and listened. He could still hear the cries and yowls, but they were growing softer; the ghast must be moving away. Maybe it hadn't seen him?

Fisher stood there, getting sand in his ear as he pressed his head against the block, listening to the world above. When fifteen minutes had passed and he still hadn't heard the terrible creature, the young villager broke the sandstone and peeked around aboveground. The desert looked clear. Glancing to the sky, he saw more clouds drifting overhead, but no tentacles were hanging down from them; it appeared to be safe.

He climbed out of the hole and continued his run to the east, toward the rising sun, its square face shining down on him and making him sweat. Ahead was a large sand dune. Picking up speed, Fisher sprinted toward the hill, leaping up the single-block jumps with practiced efficiency.

As he ran down the other side of the hill, there the sound was again: a feline cry that echoed across the desert from behind him. Glancing over his shoulder, Fisher saw the writhing tentacles of a ghast out of the corner of his eye. The monster was close, and surely had spotted him this time. Hiding underground would do no good, for the monster would just blast the sand with its fireballs and eventually uncover him. His only weapon right now was speed.

"I must make it to the village, so I can warn them about the ghasts," Fisher said in a low voice.

Ahead, he could see a desert well that stood at the top of another sandy mound. If he could make it to the well, he could jump into the waters and be safe from the monster's attacks; but he had to outrun the ghast first.

With a burst of speed, he zigzagged across the desert. A fireball exploded into the sand just to his right, leaving behind a small crater. If he had been standing there, he likely would not have survived.

Fisher leapt over a small brown bush just as another fireball struck. The brown leaves were instantly engulfed in flames as the frustrated cries of the ghast echoed across the desolate landscape.

Not bothering to look back, the villager continued to sprint, driving his body with everything he had. He wove left and right. Fisher tried to make himself a difficult target to hit. Fireballs landed all around him, some of them singeing his armor.

BLAST!

A fireball struck the ground right next to him. Terrifying fingers of fire grasped at his arm, burning away part of his smock and scorching his armor. Pain radiated up his arm and shoulder as Fisher flashed red, taking damage. The lanky NPC could feel his HP decreasing, and that had been just a glancing hit. If a fireball struck him head on . . . he was a goner.

"If I can make it to the well, I'll be safe," he said in a low voice, hoping the words would motivate his legs; they didn't.

Fisher's legs started to burn and ache as his energy reserves were slowly consumed. Gasps of hot desert air wheezed in and out of his chest and he struggled for breath. He was exhausted, but quitting was not an option.

One of his legs began to cramp. Pain of a different kind shot through his body as his HP plummeted from sheer fatigue. His sprint slowed to a run as the ghast gradually gained on him. The large sand dune now loomed before him; the well was only twenty steps away. With a burst of speed, he shot up the hill, timing his jumps so he would not falter or slow. Glancing over his shoulder, he could see the ghast had almost caught up. Fisher tried to move even faster, but his legs felt as if they were made out of iron, his feet stumbling on the edge of blocks.

"I have to keep going!"

He drew on the last bit of energy. He could feel his HP dropping as his hunger became dangerously low, but he couldn't stop now. The desert well was only eight blocks away.

"I think I'm gonna make it," he said aloud to the empty desert.

Casting another glance behind, he saw there were now two ghasts; he could practically feel them breathing on his neck. He leapt up blocks of sand, getting closer and closer as more balls of flaming death streaked through the dry desert air, each one just barely missing him.

"I'm almost there!" he said in a loud jubilant voice.

Suddenly, a ghast with bright-red eyes rose up from the other side of the sand dune right in front of him, a booming laugh coming from his vile mouth. The monster had a vile, evil look to it as if it were born out of hate and violence.

"Not close enough, fool!" the ghast shouted with glee.

The monster spat a flaming ball at the villager, striking him in the shoulder and knocking him off-balance. The ghast rose high in the air and laughed.

"I am Malacoda, the king of the ghasts," the monster boomed. "I will be the last thing you ever see."

Fisher struggled to stand, feigning injury, then leapt up into the air. He landed on the edge of the desert well and dove down into the cool waters. The other ghasts fired down on the structure, their fire-balls smashing into the roof and shredding it to dust.

While underwater and holding his breath, Fisher used his pickaxe to dig through the wall of the well and create a tiny pocket of air. He could hear the other ghasts yowling in rage as they rained more balls of fire down on the structure. They hit the watery surface and were extinguished instantly. More of the deadly spheres smashed into the well, chipping away at the cobblestone overhead, the water protecting the structure underground. In his tiny pocket of air, he waited to see if the ghasts would eventually be convinced he was destroyed.

A deafening silence filled his ears as he sat in the cool water and waited for some kind of signal that it was safe. Finally, he emerged from the well. The roof was completely obliterated, and pieces of stone and wood were strewn around the hilltop. To the east, a line of ghasts hung in the air between him and the desert village. There was no way he would ever reach Carver and the others now. Pulling out an apple, he ate it quickly, then consumed some bread until his hunger bar was full, allowing his HP to begin regenerating.

"I can't go to the village now, the ghasts will see me for sure," Fisher said to the barren landscape. "But I'm not sure I want to go running through the desert in the daylight with all those monsters floating around. I'm sorry, Carver, and everyone in the desert village, but I just can't get to you to give warning. You're on your own."

Fisher sighed, uncertain and afraid. Pulling out his pickaxe and shovel, he carved out a seat in the well, and sat in the water, chest high, waiting for night to come.

CHAPTER 4

CLOUDS

Herobrine stood atop the tallest of the Dragon's Teeth, his eyes blazing a harsh white as his frustration grew. The rocky peak stood high above the few clouds nearby. The terribly clear blue sky shone down upon the virus, mocking him with its pure cerulean color.

To the west, the sky was slowly fading to a rusty orange as a bright-red line painted the horizon. The sun was sinking below the horizon, allowing a few stars to peek down upon the Overworld from the east. Soon, the sun would disappear completely for the day, drawing a blanket of darkness across the land; it would be monster time in Minecraft. Recently, Herobrine had modified the code governing zombies and skeletons, making them impervious to the deadly rays of the sun. Now these monsters could walk about in the middle of the day without fear of bursting into flames. As far as Herobrine was concerned, that made *every* time monster time.

Herobrine glanced around at his surroundings from his perch high atop Dragon's Teeth. There were monsters milling about down below—not as many as he wanted, but he knew how to solve that problem. The real issue right now was the ghasts. The evil shadow-crafter knew these floating monsters were the key to destroying that pathetic blacksmith and taking over Minecraft once and for all. The problem was he could only infect a few of them at once with his vile hatred, and the slow pace of his progress infuriated him.

"I am Herobrine," the Maker yelled to the darkening sky. "I should be able to infect anything I want, as quickly as I want to!"

But at the moment, since the sky was clear and there were no clouds nearby, that meant there were no ghasts within his reach, and this made him even angrier. His eyes grew bright with fury as he glared out at his surroundings, his rage about to boil over.

"I am Herobrine," he shouted. "I AM HEROBRINE!"

Suddenly, a dark form materialized, visible out of the corner of his eye. Glancing over his shoulder, he found Erebus, the king of the Endermen, standing up higher on the mountaintop, looking down at him, his eyes glowing bright red. Around him floated a purple mist of teleportation particles that slowly dissipated.

"Maker, what is the problem?" Erebus asked.

"The ghasts," Herobrine snapped, his eyes glowing bright with rage. "There are none nearby for me to transform!"

"They only can be found in the clouds," the Enderman said. "The sky right now is clear."

"I can see that, you fool," Herobrine growled. "I don't need you to tell me . . ."

He stopped his rant as an idea suddenly slithered into his evil mind.

"The clouds . . . I'll infect the clouds."

"I don't understand," Erebus said.

"I don't care what you understand," Herobrine snapped, his eyes glowing brighter.

He turned and glared at the Enderman. The dark creature annoyed him for reasons he couldn't be bothered to try to understand. Maybe it was his frustration, or the feeling of being powerless against this problem. Herobrine wasn't sure; all he knew was that he didn't want Erebus here right now. Slowly, deliberately, he reached for his sword. Instantly, the king of the Endermen teleported away in fear, materializing on the ground far below. Herobrine laughed as he glared down at his foolish minion, then turned and went back to work.

Closing his eyes, the evil creature concentrated on his crafting powers. As he focused on his malicious code-altering skills, his hands began to glow that insipid pale-yellow color he loved so much. The sickly hue slowly crept up his arms like an infectious disease. When it reached his elbows, he plunged his hands into the peak of the rocky spire. The mountain seemed to shudder at his vile touch, but Herobrine didn't care.

Concentrating with all his viral skill, he made discolored clouds slowly ooze out of the mountaintop, as if the terrain were weeping in despair. The clouds, different shapes of squares and rectangles, glowed with a faint orange radiance, tiny embers dancing about the edges. Herobrine smiled. It looked like there was some kind of fire within the center of each cloud. But in addition to the orange glow, he could also see his insipid, sickly-looking yellow aura as well.

The new, infected clouds seeped from the mountain, pushing through the air and spreading outward in all directions. Some normal clouds were approaching on the perpetual east-to-west wind. When the faintly glowing, infected clouds touched one of the normal ones, there was a tiny flash of pale-yellow light, then the pure white was replaced with a sickly-looking orange and pale yellow, glowing embers sparkling around their edges. The ghasts traveling within the normal clouds cried out in shock and fear as they were also infected, an evil look developing across their large baby-like faces.

Herobrine watched with evil glee as his virus clouds claimed more and more of the sky; his airborne troops were growing in number right before his eyes. After the infection was complete, the newly-recruited ghasts turned their angry eyes toward the Dragon's Teeth and floated toward him.

"Excellent," Herobrine mumbled. "My new slaves are arriving, just as it should be. That's one problem solved."

The moans of a small group of zombies drifted up from the ground. Glancing down, he saw Erebus standing near the lava flow that spilled down the side of one of the rocky spires. A group of Endermen stood with him, and a small collection of zombies were clustered nearby. The total number of monsters down there was pathetic. At one time, Herobrine had possessed a massive army of monsters, hundreds and hundreds of vicious creatures willing to do his bidding, but that cowardly blacksmith had destroyed them, leaving him with only a handful of survivors.

"We will have our revenge on you for that, Smithy," Herobrine hissed to himself.

Concentrating with his viral powers, the vile shadow-crafter teleported to the ground. Instantly, he appeared next to Erebus.

"Maker, I see you solved your problem," the Enderman king said. "That's excellent."

"I don't need, nor do I want, your approval!" Herobrine growled, his eyes glowing bright.

"Of course you don't, Maker," Erebus replied, lowering his red eyes to the ground.

"I have a task for you and your Endermen," Herobrine said.

"We will do as you command," the Enderman replied.

"Of course you will," Herobrine sneered. "You and the other Endermen are to teleport out into all the caves and tunnels across the Overworld. You will gather more skeletons and zombies. We need a proper army that will keep the blacksmith and his villagers sufficiently distracted, so they don't realize my real plan."

"It will be done," Erebus said, his red eyes glowing bright with excitement.

"Any monsters that refuse to volunteer shall be destroyed," Herobrine directed.

"Of course," the king of the Endermen replied.

"When we have enough monsters, we'll begin the pursuit of the blacksmith," Herobrine added. "If there are any villagers in our path, we'll destroy them, if for no other reason than because they offend me. These NPCs must be taught who is the *true* ruler of Minecraft."

"There is a desert village just on the other side of the Great Chasm," Erebus said. "Perhaps we could destroy that first?"

"No, I have other plans for them," Herobrine said.

The Maker's eyes then began to glow bright white as he thought about what would soon happen to that village. *If only the blacksmith were there when it happened,* he thought, then laughed a maniacal, evil laugh.

CHAPTER 5

SAVANNA VILLAGE

The NPC army reached the exit of Two-sword Pass just as the sun was setting gracefully on the western horizon. Gameknight glanced up at the rosy sky and knew they would need to be extra cautious as they ran through the night. But from what he'd seen since travelling into the distant past of Minecraft, the time of the Great Zombie Invasion, zombies and skeletons curiously did not burn in the sun. That strange difference from the present day made daytime just as dangerous as the night. The User-that-is-not-a-user had a hunch it had something to do with Herobrine, somehow.

Many of the villagers breathed a sigh of relief when they left the sandy desert behind. Half of the army had come from a village in the savanna nearby, and those warriors looked forward to being with their families again. Gameknight knew how anxious they must be to see the familiar walls and buildings of their villages; in fact, NPCs always felt safer in *any* village, even when it wasn't their own. But Gameknight also knew that their party's urge to hurry should not replace their sense of caution. There were still monsters about.

The NPC army passed through an extreme hills biome and into a forest landscape. They ran quietly through the dense growth of trees, the branches and leaves blocking out the slowly darkening sky. Gameknight glanced skyward, still on the lookout for ghasts, but fortunately, all he could see through the open spaces of the leafy canopy were stars; the sky was clear.

Breathing a sigh of relief, the User-that-is-not-a-user shifted his attention to their surroundings. With the overhead threat seemingly absent, he concentrated on the possibility of an ambush by the ground-dwelling monsters of the Overworld.

"Keep your eyes peeled," Gameknight whispered. "Pass the word, but stay as quiet as possible."

Fencer relayed the message, then turned back to the User-that-is-not-a-user.

"You think there might actually be monsters out here?" Fencer asked. "We destroyed a big chunk of Herobrine's army in that last battle near the Great Chasm. I imagine Herobrine will be hiding somewhere, licking his wounds and feeling sorry for himself."

"Herobrine doesn't feel sorry for anyone," Gameknight said. "He's completely without pity or remorse. It makes no difference to him how many monsters were destroyed in that battle, because he doesn't value anything other than his own evil existence. If he thinks he can hurt us with an attack, then he will definitely try."

Wilbur suddenly stopped and raised his nose into the air, sniffing. He glanced up at Gameknight999 and oinked quietly, his tiny black eyes narrowing.

A clicking sound filled the air. Gameknight held a hand up into the air, then stopped and listened. The rest of the army froze where they stood, some of them quietly drawing weapons from their inventories.

The clicking was getting louder. That could only mean one thing: spiders were approaching, and it sounded like they were coming from the southwest. Gameknight motioned for one group of archers to set up in a line, then for more of them to climb up into the trees. He then directed swordsmen to stand behind the archers.

"Warriors, protect the archers," Gameknight whispered as he positioned his troops.

The spiders now sounded like a storm of crickets, their clicking flooding the air. He couldn't see them yet, but he knew there were a lot of them.

"Everyone get ready," the User-that-is-not-a-user whispered. "They're almost here."

"I don't see anything," one of the archers said. "Where are . . ."

The villager stopped in mid-sentence as glowing red eyes suddenly appeared in the distance. Like a massive swarm of red fireflies, the clusters of eight glowing eyes moved closer, all bright and filled with hatred. Now the warriors could tell there were a lot of the fuzzy monsters approaching.

"Wait until they get close," Gameknight whispered. "We can't let any of them get away."

The fuzzy black monstrosities continued forward, and Gameknight realized that they weren't even aware of the villagers' presence near them. But then, just as the User-that-is-not-a-user thought they might take them completely by surprise, someone dropped a sword. The blade clattered against an iron boot, making a clank that sounded like thunder in comparison to the silence of the forest. The clicking of the spiders surged in volume as the monsters charged.

"Here they come!" Gameknight shouted, the need for silence now gone. "Wait . . . wait . . . now, FIRE!"

The archers aimed for the clusters of red eyes, letting their arrows soar into the night and disappear into the dark forest where the spiders were gathered. Just then, a silver light bathed the landscape as the full moon finally rose above the horizon and lit the Overworld. The spiders were easily visible now. The archers fired as fast as they could, their bowstrings humming like a symphony orchestra.

"Fencer!" Gameknight shouted.

The NPC ran to his side.

"Take the swordsmen on the left flank and go behind the spiders," Gameknight explained. "I'll take the ones on the right. We must surround the monsters. None can be allowed to escape. If they do, they will tell Herobrine our location. We don't want that . . . not yet."

Fencer didn't reply. He just nodded his head and ran to the warriors on the left, while Gameknight did the same on the right. As the archers kept the spiders distracted, the soldiers moved around the large group of monsters, then closed in. Pulling out their own bows, the swordsmen suddenly became archers and fired on the monsters from all sides.

The dark fuzzy creatures realized their mistake; they were surrounded. With no hope of escape, the monsters fought ferociously. They charged toward the archers, their mandibles clicking wildly. Wicked curved claws swiped at NPCs, trying to tear at their HP. Many of the archers dropped their bows and drew their swords for combat in close quarters. Quickly, the battle degraded from a carefully-orchestrated dance of spider and villager to a chaotic melee of hand-to-claw fighting.

Gameknight dropped his bow and drew his two swords, then charged into the fray.

"FOR MINECRAFT!" he yelled.

He smashed into the spider formation, his razor-sharp blades swinging wildly. Slashing to the left and swinging to the right, the User-that-is-not-a-user, masquerading as Smithy of the Two-swords, tore into the fuzzy bodies with a fury.

"Protect your neighbor and fight together!" Gameknight shouted as he blocked a claw from hitting a builder next to him. "Everyone push forward!"

The NPCs advanced, pushing the spiders back, but because they were surrounded, it only drove the spiders into a tighter and tighter clump. Soon, the monsters were so close to each other it made fighting difficult for them, and even easier for the archers perched in the treetops. Pointed shafts rained down upon the fuzzy creatures like a deadly thunderstorm, causing many of the monsters to disappear quickly as the last of their HP was extinguished.

In minutes, the last of the spiders were gone. The villagers cheered, but Gameknight held his hand up, asking for silence as he glanced around at the shadowy forest.

"There could still be more around," the User-that-is-not-a-user warned. "We must be careful."

The villagers nodded as they collected their arrows that had missed targets and were stuck in the ground or in trees.

"Archers, out of the trees," Gameknight said. "We need to get to the savanna village before we run across any more unpleasant surprises."

The army reformed, and began to travel with haste toward the distant village. As they sprinted, Fencer moved up next to Gameknight999.

"That was a great battle," the NPC said. "We didn't lose anyone."

The User-that-is-not-a-user shook his head. Fencer looked as if he had actually enjoyed the engagement, but for Gameknight, it had been terrifying. He hated being the sole person to decide what they were to do, which strategy to employ, which group should attack and who should be held in reserve. The responsibility felt like a two-ton weight on his square shoulders.

"Nothing makes a battle great," Gameknight corrected. "The only way to make a battle great is to avoid it entirely. Violence only causes more violence."

"But at least there are a few less spiders about," Fencer said.

"Perhaps, but one thing concerns me."

"What's that?"

They swerved around a cluster of bushes, Gameknight going to the left as Fencer moved to the right.

"Herobrine is rebuilding his army," the User-that-is-not-a-user continued. "Those spiders were heading to their queen, Shaikulud."

"How do you know that?" Fencer asked. "Maybe they were just moving across the land and had the misfortune to run into us."

"Because spiders don't work or stay together unless they absolutely must," Gameknight explained. "Spiders are solitary creatures. These were moving together in a small group when they could have been all spread out. No, they were definitely acting as an intentional team." He sighed. "It was a mistake for us to disband the army. The war is clearly not over. We will be in need of Carver and his warriors before long."

"What is it with you and wars?" another villager asked.

Gameknight turned to face Butcher, a villager who had likely come from the savannah village they were heading toward right now; he'd been with the group for as long as Gameknight could remember, back when the real Smithy was still around.

"You *always* seem to think there is a war brewing. We just defeated Herobrine, again. Don't you think he's had enough?"

"That evil virus will never be satisfied until he destroys everyone and everything," Gameknight explained. "And now he can attack with ghasts, from the sky. The defenses around our villages are going to be useless."

"We'll see," Butcher replied. "When you see my village in the savanna, look at our defenses and you tell me if you think they're useless."

The army ran on in silence until they reached the end of the forest and passed into the savanna. The lush green of the forest was replaced with a gray-green grass that stretched out before them. Strange trees dotted the landscape, each one bent and distorted in different ways, giving a unique look to each.

Gameknight loved the acacia trees in this biome. He thought they looked as if they were stopped in the middle of some kind of dance, each tree expressing itself in a distinctive way. At the top of a large hill, just at the edge of their vision, he could barely make out the village. The sight made the army move faster, all of them eager to get to safety.

They sprinted across the rolling hills of the savanna, the heat of the biome making the NPCs' iron armor grow hot. Gameknight was glad he still wore the dark-brown leather armor that Smithy had on when he'd been killed. Many times, villagers had offered him a set of iron armor, but he felt he needed to continue wearing the leather armor to keep the disguise intact. The only iron he wore was his helmet, the large nosepiece covering his small, user-like nose. No doubt, if he removed the helmet, the other villagers would instantly see he did not have the bulbous nose of an NPC and his true identity would be revealed. As a result, he kept the iron helmet on at all times.

As they climbed the hill upon which the village sat, Gameknight noticed there were no guards on the walls. The archer towers seemed strangely absent of archers, and the gates to the village were wide open. He stopped on a wide plateau that sat before the community.

"Where are all the soldiers?" Gameknight asked. "Butcher, what's going on?"

"I don't know," the NPC replied as he moved to the blacksmith's side. "When we left the village to join you in battle, the mothers stayed behind to take care of the children, and the elderly remained to stand guard on the walls and watchtowers. Now they seem to all be gone."

"I don't like this," Fencer said.

"Nor do I," Gameknight said. "I fear something has happened."

He glanced around at the other NPCs and saw the same expression on all their blocky faces: fear.

CHAPTER 6

SURPRISE

They approached the village walls quickly and quietly. There were massive fortifications standing eight blocks high, with alternating blocks along the top for archers to use as cover. Holes were cut into the walls with trapdoors covering the opening. They could be easily flipped open from inside, allowing more access for archers. Towers loomed on the corners of the wall standing another eight blocks higher, with openings on the sides to allow archers a clear field of fire. It was an impressive display; likely, this fortress was impregnable from ground forces. But from the air, Gameknight realized looking at it . . . it was vulnerable.

He moved to the wall and approached the open doors that should have been closed, especially since night had fallen. No movement was visible within the village.

This is not good, Gameknight thought.

Slowly, he drew his diamond sword with his right hand and the iron blade with his left. Turning, he looked at the other villagers. They all had the same concerned expressions on their square faces: something was wrong. Gameknight moved next to Fencer and Butcher and spoke in a low voice.

"Here's what I want to do," Gameknight said. "Swordsmen, go in first and form a battle line. Archers, go in behind and place blocks on the ground so they can fire over the heads of the front line. One company of swordsmen will go to the left flank, and another to the right, to protect our sides." He glanced around at their worried faces, watching as fear slowly changed to rage. "Don't worry, we'll get in there and find out what happened to our people."

"I have the feeling they're okay," one of the NPCs said. Gameknight looked at his smock and instantly recognized him as a carpenter.

"What?" Butcher asked, an angry tone to his voice.

"I said I think everyone is okay," Carpenter repeated. "So don't start shooting right away."

"Why do you think they're okay?" the User-that-is-not-a-user asked.

"Well . . . umm . . . I sorta had a dream about it before we left the desert village," Carpenter explained. "It was a strange dream, like I really *was* back in the village. But anyway, I saw everyone there, and I think they're all safe."

"A dream . . . that's impossible," Fencer said with a laugh. "You're an NPC. We don't remember our dreams. None of us do. Maybe you were just exhausted from the battle and hallucinating."

"I only know what I remember," Carpenter said, "and it was a dream, a strange but real dream."

"Well, no offense, but I think I'll just trust my sword first and your dreams second," Butcher said.

"Those are my people in there, and I'm gonna find out what happened, and punish those responsible, if even a single villager is hurt."

He turned to Gameknight, Butcher's black hair hung across one eye. He reached up and pushed the wayward strands back into place.

"Let's do this," the NPC growled.

"Okay, everybody, run as quietly as possible," Gameknight said. "Now!"

The NPCs darted toward the village, swordsmen in the front and on the sides, archers at the back. They swept through the village gates, each warrior's nerves stretched to its limits. But as soon as they stopped and began setting up their defenses, loud shouts rose up from behind buildings and through open windows. Mothers and children and grandparents all ran forth with flowers in their hands, celebrating the return of their friends and family.

The warriors immediately relaxed as they put away their weapons and ran to embrace their spouses and friends. Many wives and grandparents wept upon learning their loved ones had not returned from the war. The cost of stopping Herobrine had been severe, and many families had been shattered in order to keep Minecraft safe; now they were beginning to pay the price that would haunt some of them for a long, long time.

Walking through the village, Gameknight consoled those that grieved, many of whom he didn't really know. But they all knew Smithy, the blacksmith leader of this army. So Gameknight continued to play the part, though living the lie still nagged at him. He wanted to come clean and tell them all the truth, but the User-that-is-not-a-user was afraid they would turn on him. Gameknight finally felt like he was a part of the community; he didn't want to lose that.

Am I just being selfish? he thought. *Wouldn't the truth be better, regardless of the consequences?*

Gameknight shook his head as he contemplated these questions. He wasn't sure what the right thing to do was, so instead he focused on what could be done, now, to help others, and that was to console those that mourned their lost loved ones.

As he moved through the village, he found Carpenter standing off to the side, watching both the celebration around them as well as the sadness. Something about the NPC's story earlier bothered Gameknight.

"Carpenter, you mentioned a dream," the User-that-is-not-a-user said.

The tall, skinny NPC looked over at Gameknight with warm hazel eyes that seemed to sparkle with golden embers in the moonlight. He was unusually tall and skinny for a villager, with dark-brown hair that was thinning across the top of his square head.

"I didn't really want to talk about it, but I felt it was important to say out there on the grassy plain," Carpenter explained.

"You said it was a dream, but it felt real?" Gameknight asked.

Carpenter nodded his square head, his short-cropped hair bobbing up and down.

"Can you tell me more about what it was like?"

"Sure," Carpenter replied. "The first strange thing about the dream was the fog; there was a silvery mist that seemed to wrap over everything. I could feel the moisture in the mist and it was incredibly cold. But then it began to fade away and

I saw the village. Everyone was sleeping and had a transparent sort of look to them, but every now and then, an NPC would turn solid, as if they were really there with me. I thought they could see me for just an instant, but then they'd fade again, and only their transparent, sleeping body would remain." The tall NPC lowered his voice and moved closer. "I know it sounds crazy, but I think the dream was real. I think it was trying to tell me something."

And then Gameknight realized what Carpenter was talking about. Suddenly, he remembered his friend Crafter telling him about a distant great-great uncle from a hundred years in his past, which, of course, was now Gameknight's present.

"I'm sure no one believes you about dreaming, because NPCs don't realize they dream," Gameknight said. "They never remember their dreams, but I know you do. I believe you."

The tall villager relaxed and finally smiled.

"What you experienced is called the Land of Dreams," Gameknight explained. "You're a Dream Walker, and I am as well."

"You mean you dream too?" Carpenter asked.

"Not for a while, but I've learned how to control the dreams, so that I can go into the Land of Dreams whenever I want."

"Really?"

Gameknight nodded.

"I can teach you this skill," the User-that-is-not-a-user explained. "But you must realize there are dangers in the Land of Dreams. Some of the monsters can go into the dream world, and their claws are just as sharp as they are in the real world. It is important for you to know: if you die in the Land of Dreams, you die in Minecraft. So you must be careful."

Carpenter smiled and put an arm around Gameknight's shoulder and gave him a hug.

"Smithy, I've been struggling to understand these dreams since the . . . awakening," Carpenter said. "Finally, I can make some sense of this."

"Just remember, there are real dangers there in that silvery mist," Gameknight warned. "You must always be careful."

The tall NPC nodded and gave the blacksmith another smile, then moved off to join the celebration. Glancing across the courtyard, he saw the Oracle smiling at him as she tapped her cane on the ground, but then the smile changed to a scowl as if she'd just sensed something dangerous. The User-that-is-not-a-user thought he heard the faint cry of a ghast, just barely audible and far, far away, but he wasn't sure; it could have been his exhausted imagination. By the look on the Oracle's wrinkled face, Gameknight was sure something in Minecraft had changed.

He glanced up at a small cloud that was floating by and sensed trouble, but not in the fluffy rectangle high in the air. Instead, the trouble he felt was far away, like a distant storm, but it was approaching . . . fast.

"What are you up to, Herobrine?" Gameknight said to himself. "I know you're planning something, but what?"

Weaver ran up to him and grabbed him by the arm.

"Come on Smithy, the celebration is starting," the young boy said, his bright blue eyes sparkling with excitement. Gameknight shook his head to clear his thoughts, and allowed himself to be led toward the celebration, even though he kept a wary eye skyward.

CHAPTER 7

LAND OF DREAMS

Gameknight had gone to bed soon after the celebration got underway. He was exhausted, not just from running through the desert, through the forest, and into the savanna, but also from the stress of responsibility. The User-that-is-not-a-user was continually afraid that he'd do something wrong that would get someone hurt, or worse. He had to make all the decisions and come up with their plans all by himself. If his decisions were wrong and someone died that wasn't supposed to, it could alter the future and hurt his friends as well. This responsibility and constant state of fear was exhausting and wearing him out. But when Gameknight's head finally rested on a pillow, much of that fatigue disappeared as his eyelids grew heavier and heavier until . . .

The mist wrapped around his ankles like a murky bog, clinging to him as if afraid to let go. It was wet and cold, like a blanket left out in the rain overnight. There was a silvery sheen to the mist, as if it were shining from within, the damp fog appearing almost magical. Instantly, Gameknight999 knew this was the Land of Dreams. It had been a while since he'd been here. The last time had been long ago when he'd battled Erebus, the king of the Endermen, on the steps of the Source, with his friends Hunter and Stitcher at his side. And now he was back again . . . and because he was in the past, Erebus was still alive!

Gameknight had the faintest memory of Crafter mentioning his great-great uncle, Carpenter. His friend had said his ancestor was the first Dream Walker, the first to ever enter the Land of Dreams. He knew there had been many more throughout the history of Minecraft. His friends Hunter and Stitcher had both been Dream Walkers, and, of course, Gameknight himself was as well. Their job was to protect the NPCs from the monsters that prowl in the ethereal world.

Gameknight knew that typically, NPCs didn't dream, or more accurately, they didn't remember their dreams. As they began to fall asleep, villagers tended to pass through the Land of Dreams before they became completely submerged into their sleeping mind. And at that point, while they were transitioning from consciousness to fully asleep, they would materialize in the Land of Dreams and would be vulnerable to the monsters that preyed in the silvery mists. It was the Dream Walker's job to protect the villagers and ensure everyone was safe.

As the cold, silvery mist cleared, Gameknight could see the village around him. The structures all appeared to be solid, but he knew he could pass through them if he focused his mind. Like in a dream, things were only as real as you imagined them to be.

He walked through the village, moving through the walls of homes and peering through windows, making sure everyone was safe. Occasionally, he saw the sleeping form of an NPC. Those that were awake and those that were completely asleep had a transparent look to them, but the ones that moved from wakefulness to sleep took on a solid form for just a few moments, then became transparent again.

Focusing his mind on the desert village near Dragon's Teeth, Gameknight999 teleported at the speed of thought. Instantly, he was standing at the center of the sandy village. The cobblestone walls that they'd built still stood strong around the village, with translucent villagers walking along the battlements, watching for monsters. He moved out into the desert and found it empty, save for the ever-diligent cacti standing guard over the scorched landscape. There were no monsters nearby, but for some reason, he had a feeling something dangerous was approaching.

Glancing up at the sky, the User-that-is-not-a-user could see stars sparkling like shining gems sewn into a dark tapestry that stretched from horizon to horizon. Clouds were drifting toward the village from the east, but for some reason, they seemed to glow and sparkle as if burning embers were bouncing about within the fluffy rectangles. As they neared the village, a bright ball of fire streaked down toward the NPCs on the fortified wall. It smashed into the cobblestone, tearing a gigantic hole into the fortification as if some kind of giant had just taken a bite out of it. The warriors that had been standing atop the battlements were gone, consumed in the flames.

Another fireball fell from the sparkling clouds. It struck the blacksmith's home, causing hungry flames to lick up the walls of the wooden structure, quickly covering the rest of the side and the roof.

Gameknight yelled up at the clouds, but he couldn't do anything; he was in the Land of Dreams, and all this was happening in the real world. Villagers ran about, grabbing buckets and filling them with water, then throwing it on the flames. But that was exactly what the ghasts wanted: to draw the NPCs out. More fireballs fell on the village, but instead of hitting the structures, they were aimed at those with buckets, consuming their HP in seconds.

"I have to do something," Gameknight cried.

Quickly, he closed his eyes and concentrated on Carver. Instantly, the User-that-is-not-a-user appeared in his house, the stocky NPC still asleep. But as the noise grew, the NPC stirred and began to wake. As he moved from asleep to awake, he passed through the transition zone again and solidified.

"Carver, get the people to the crafting chamber," Gameknight said. "You understand me. Ghasts are attacking . . . get to the crafting chamber, get to the crafting chamber, get to the . . ."

Carver became transparent again as he woke, no longer able to hear Gameknight. He pulled out his shining axe and stepped out of his house. Gameknight followed, unsure as to whether his warning had even registered to his friend in his groggy state. A feline cry floated down from overhead. It was an angry sound, as if some kind of cat-like baby was bemoaning its hatred for those on the ground.

Gameknight watched as Carver surveyed the situation, then began shouting to the other villagers.

"Get to the crafting chamber!" he screamed as he ran throughout the village.

A fireball shot toward him. He turned just in time to bat it away. The burning sphere bounced off his axe and flew through the air, striking another ghast that was floating off to the left. The monster wailed in pain, then turned and faced the source of the attack. But Carver knew standing still was never a good idea in battle. He was already moving, running back along the cobblestone wall, searching for villagers to help.

Those who survived were now gathering in the cobblestone watchtower. They flowed, one after another, down the ladder that led to the crafting chamber, which sat at least twenty layers under the surface, if not deeper. With that much stone and sand and dirt between them and the destructive ghasts, the NPCs would likely be safe.

The storm of fireballs increased as more ghasts emerged from the glowing clouds, each with a malicious look on their pale, white face. Gameknight thought about his favorite bow, the one with Infinity, Power V, and Flame. Suddenly, it appeared in his hand. Drawing back an arrow, he fired at the closest monster, but, of course, his flaming arrow passed right through the beast; the ghasts were not in the Land of Dreams like he was. His weapons were useless against them.

All Gameknight999 could do was watch in horror as the floating beasts flattened building after building. Suddenly, Carver ran out of the cobblestone watchtower. He dodged fireball after fireball as he shot into a small home engulfed in flames. Seconds later, he ran out with an elderly woman in his arms. Gameknight could tell the old woman was terribly ill and likely could not walk, with green spirals floating around her as if she had been poisoned.

Carver ran through the village, weaving to the left and right, making himself a difficult target to hit. A fireball exploded nearby, singeing his left sleeve, but he did not pause to extinguish the smoldering fabric. Instead, he dashed for the door of the watchtower.

Right behind him, a stream of fireballs crashed against the wooden door, blowing it to smithereens. Gameknight teleported to the watchtower and caught a glimpse of the stocky NPC dropping the woman into a hole in the corner of the building. Gameknight was shocked as she fell through the vertical shaft, but was relieved when he finally heard a splash at the bottom; they'd put water at the bottom of the passage to cushion her fall. Carver climbed down the tunnel just as another cluster of fireballs crashed into the watchtower, tearing a huge piece out of the side.

Gameknight teleported to the top of the watchtower and surveyed the damage as more flaming spheres smashed into the bottom of the structure. The cobblestone wall at the front of the village was completely destroyed, though no monsters were taking advantage of the breach and pouring through the opening. Multiple buildings burned as bright tongues of flame licked up walls and across roofs, casting flickering orange light on the rest of the village. Explosions of fire dotted the surroundings as the attacks continued, each one punctuated with a baby-like cry or feline yowl.

At least a dozen ghasts now floated overhead, looking for targets. When they saw all the villagers were gone, they took out their rage on the buildings themselves, burning everything that stood within the cobblestone walls. A fireball streaked straight toward Gameknight999. He knew he could not be hurt, but instinctively drew his diamond sword and tried to knock the flaming ball of fire away. Instead, it whooshed right through him, as if he wasn't there, and smashed into the top of the watchtower behind Gameknight, destroying the stone bricks.

Gameknight teleported to the ground, then moved to a large sand dune that stood outside the village. He watched as the ghasts destroyed every last building, then went to work on the fortified walls. The very ground where the village stood began to glow as the heat from the fires seeped into the stone and sand. The floating monsters left nothing standing, firing their balls of death at anything that still resembled the village that had once stood there.

Teleporting to the crafting chamber deep underground, the User-that-is-not-a-user breathed a sigh of relief when he materialized in the large cavern. There he found villagers, shaken and scared, but alive. Some mourned the loss of loved ones, but nearly all of the NPCs had survived the attack . . . this time.

Gameknight knew Herobrine's poisoning of the ghasts had just put the villagers at a huge disadvantage; they had little defense against their fireballs. What would they do now? He shuddered as he realized the balance of power had now tipped to Herobrine's side, and there was nothing the villagers could do about it, other than wait for the next attack to come from the sky. But where would Herobrine attack next?

CHAPTER 8

TO THE RESCUE

Gameknight woke with a start, suddenly lurching as if he were falling. Sweat ran along his chest and arms and sides; his shirt under the leather armor was soaked. Sitting up, he leapt out of bed and looked upward, his heart pounding in his chest. He expected to see ghasts staring down at him with their evil white faces, but as he became more awake, he realized that he was still inside, a wooden ceiling over his head.

Gathering his weapons and items from a chest, he ran out of the small wooden house, and stood next to the wall, pressing his back against the structure and staring up into the sky. It was dark, a myriad of stars sparkling down upon him through a clear, cloudless night.

Gameknight suddenly realized he'd been holding his breath. He finally exhaled, and, stepping away from the wall, he moved out into the open, ready to dart away if attacked. Everything seemed peaceful and calm, but it had seemed that way at the desert village, too . . . right up until the ghasts invaded.

Sprinting to the cobblestone watchtower, Gameknight flung open the door. He grabbed the rungs that led upward and climbed. Scaling the ladder as fast as he could, the User-that-is-not-a-user ascended to the top of the tower. When he stepped onto the roof, Gameknight999 surveyed the surroundings.

He gave a sigh of relief. In the moonlight, he could see the savanna desert was completely devoid of monsters and the sky was empty, save for the millions of sparkling stars that peered down upon the land. There was no danger nearby.

Glancing down at the village that surrounded him, the User-that-is-not-a-user realized that this village was just as vulnerable as Carver's, and was the closest one to Dragon's Teeth.

"How long until the ghasts are here?" Gameknight muttered. "It's only a matter of time."

"What'd you say, Smithy?" a skinny young NPC said.

Startled, he turned and found an NPC on the watchtower with him. He'd probably been there when Gameknight had reached the top, but he hadn't noticed him.

"You're . . ."

"Watcher, sir," the young NPC said with a grimace, as if his name was some kind of embarrassment.

The youth held a bow in his hand, an arrow notched. Gameknight could see he held it with practiced care, balancing it between his thumb and index finger instead of grabbing it with his whole hand; he held it like Hunter would, like a true archer.

"Have you seen anything funny going on out there in the savanna?" Gameknight asked.

Watcher shook his head, his long blond hair swinging back and forth across his face.

"Nope, it's quiet out there, that's for sure," the villager replied.

"Not for long," Gameknight said in a low voice, then moved to the ladder and went back to the ground.

Throwing the door to the watchtower open, he ran through the village, looking for Fencer. After the celebration, and mourning, people had opened their homes to the visitors, offering beds to let the exhausted warriors sleep. But there had been more people than beds, and the homes were not big enough to hold everyone. To solve this problem, beds had been set up all throughout the village, along the fortified walls, near the fields, around the central well . . . anywhere there was room.

Gameknight knew Fencer would likely have been the last to stop celebrating, and would probably not be in a house. So he ran through the village, checking all the beds that lay under the stars, finding tired warriors stretched out in each, but not the one he was looking for. Glancing to the east, the User-that-is-not-a-user noticed the sky was beginning to glow a deep red, then slowly faded to an orange, the sun almost ready to peek up over the horizon. Gradually, the curtain of night was pulled back as small groups of villagers woke, ready to greet the day.

Sprinting toward the front gates, Gameknight finally found Fencer in a cot near the fortified wall.

"Fencer, get up!" Gameknight shouted. "Everyone, get up!"

"What is it?" the balding NPC said, the gray circle of hair around his ever-expanding scalp almost glowing in the crimson light of dawn.

"Carver's desert village . . . it's been destroyed!" the User-that-is-not-a-user exclaimed.

"What?!" Fencer said, sitting up quickly. "How do you know this?"

"I was able to see it in the Land of Dreams."

"What are you talking about?" Fencer asked. "Are you telling me you had a dream and *that's* what you're excited about?"

"It's more complicated than that," Gameknight tried to explain, but Fencer was already laying back down on his bed, going back to sleep.

"Weaver . . . I need to find Weaver and Carpenter," he muttered to himself.

Dashing through the village, he hunted for the two NPCs, shouting out their names as loud as he could. Something terrible had happened in the desert, and he didn't care whom he woke. Finally, they emerged from buildings to see what all the commotion was about.

"Weaver, the ghasts have destroyed Carver's village in the desert."

"What?!" the young boy exclaimed.

He turned toward Carpenter, and noticed that the tall, skinny NPC looked confused.

"I saw it in the Land of Dreams," Gameknight said. "The ghasts destroyed the village, but I was able to warn them. They went into the crafting chamber and survived, but their village is gone. I'm going out into the desert to bring them back here. We must get the village ready for an attack from the air . . . from ghasts. We need buckets of water and . . ." He went through a litany of things they needed to do before he returned. "No doubt this village will be targeted next," Gameknight said.

Now Fencer was up again and approaching. Gameknight turned to him.

"The village must be prepared for an aerial assault," the User-that-is-not-a-user explained. "These cobblestone walls will do nothing. They didn't help Carver and the desert village, and they won't help here, either. Get everyone ready. Carpenter knows what to do."

He turned and faced the tall villager.

"Carpenter, it's vital the diggers get working on a chamber underground. That's the only chance everyone has in case the battle doesn't go well. We don't know where the ghasts will strike, so we must hope for the best, but prepare for the worst."

"Understood," Carpenter said. "We'll be ready."

Gameknight gave him a nod, then ran the gates.

"Ahh . . . Smithy, where are you going?" Fencer asked.

"I'm heading back into the desert. Carver and the others need help."

"We're going to lead them back here," Weaver said as he moved to Gameknight's side.

"Oink," Wilbur confirmed.

"Well, you aren't going alone," Fencer replied.

"I need you here to help get everything prepared," Gameknight explained.

"Then I'll send some soldiers with you," Fencer said.

"Okay. I'll wait five minutes, then I'm leaving."

Fencer ran off, collecting warriors from all across the village. In three minutes, he returned with two dozen soldiers. Gameknight checked everyone's inventories, making sure they all had plenty of arrows. When he finished the inspection, the User-that-is-not-a-user found the Oracle and four of her light-crafters standing nearby, ready to accompany him.

"What are you doing?" he asked the old woman.

"We're going with you," the Oracle said in a scratchy voice. "This has the touch of that evil virus, Herobrine, all over it. I'm the anti-virus. We're going with you."

The Oracle had been sent into Minecraft after someone in the physical world, probably the developer of Minecraft, Notch, had detected the presence of the virus, Herobrine. To balance things out and make Minecraft stable, an anti-virus program had been added to Minecraft's software, but when it arrived, it had been "awakened," like all the villagers, and become alive. That anti-virus program was the Oracle, and her tools in the software battle with Herobrine were her light-crafters.

"Are you sure you're up to going back out there into the desert?" Gameknight asked. "We'll have to move fast, and it's gonna be difficult."

The Oracle took a step closer to Gameknight999, a scowl etched on her square, wrinkled face. It seemed as if she grew taller, somehow.

"Just because I look like an old woman, that doesn't mean I'm frail," she said in a scratchy voice. "You of all people should know it's not wise to judge people only by their appearance."

The User-that-is-not-a-user took a step back and lowered his head.

"You're right," he replied.

Other than Fencer, the Oracle was the only person who knew he was posing as Smithy, and was not really the blacksmith.

"Sorry," Gameknight added sheepishly.

"It's all right, child," the Oracle said with a kind, grandmotherly smile that reminded Gameknight of his own grandmother, Gramma GG.

Some of the other NPCs giggled at their leader's discomfort. But when the Oracle cast her ancient gaze on them, they all fell silent.

"Enough," the Oracle snapped. "I, too, sensed what happened out there in the desert. We must not be delayed."

"Okay, everyone ready?" Gameknight asked. The warriors nodded their boxy heads. "The villagers out there need our help, and we're going to give it. I'll explain more on the way."

"SMITHY!" they shouted.

"Then let's go."

Gameknight reached out and opened the wooden doors set in the cobblestone wall, then ran out into the savanna, a line of armored NPCs following close behind. He wasn't certain what Herobrine would try next, but thoughts of what *might* happen began to circle around in his head.

What if there are ghasts waiting for us? Gameknight thought. *What if the attack on the desert village was just a ploy to draw us out? What if he still has a zombie army somewhere out there? I have to come up with a plan on my own, again, and hope it doesn't get everyone hurt . . . or worse.*

Focus on what you can do now, child, another thought said in his mind. *"What-if's" will only devour your courage, and we can't have that, can we?*

Gameknight cast a glance to the Oracle who was running next to him, a knowing smile on her old and wrinkled face.

"I forgot you can hear my thoughts," the User-that-is-not-a-user said softly.

She smiled.

He nodded.

I'll focus on what we can *do,* Gameknight thought, *and that's finding our friends as quickly as possible.*

The Oracle smiled again as soft, soothing music filled the air; the music of Minecraft. Gameknight saw it made all the villagers relax a little, the tension and uncertainty of what they were about to do slipping silently from their minds.

But as they ran, a nagging fear that Gameknight could not identify nibbled at the back of his mind. He was forgetting something, and whatever it was, it was dangerous.

CHAPTER 9

GATHERING FORCES

The sound of running water echoed across one side of the massive cavern, while the smell of ash and the constant sound of bubbling, molten stone filled the other. The sorrowful moans of decaying zombies and the clattering of skeleton bones added to the acoustics, creating a tapestry of sounds and smells that permeated the large subterranean enclosure.

Herobrine walked through the cavern, his eyes glowing bright white with evil excitement, casting harsh spotlights of illumination wherever he gazed. Craters dotted every inch of the uneven floor; they were scars from the explosive creation of the zombie-town by his army of creepers. A single HP fountain threw a cascade of sparkling green embers into the air that arced gracefully, then fell to the rough ground again, feeding the zombies that stood under the emerald shower with rejuvenating HP.

The Maker smiled.

He knew the creepers had not joined his army just to be sacrificed, their explosive lives used only to carve out this hollow in the rocks. But that didn't matter to Herobrine. The creepers, as with all of the monsters in the Overworld, were his to command, his to use, and his to discard—violently, if necessary. This large zombie-town, replete with a sparkling green HP fountain at the center, was necessary in his campaign against the villagers, and the creepers served their purpose. But now, Oxus, the king of the creepers, had taken his forces and gone into hiding somewhere in the Overworld. They were no longer willing to participate in this historic struggle. No matter. Herobrine knew he could do this without those child-like creepers and their arrogant king.

Suddenly, an Enderman appeared before him, a mist of purple teleportation particles shrouding his identity. But as the lavender fog cleared, a dark red skin, like the color of dried blood, showed through the mist, as well as a pair of red eyes glowing bright.

"Erebus, what have you to report?" Herobrine asked.

"My Endermen are bringing the monsters here, just as you commanded," the shadowy monster said.

"What did you say?" the Maker asked, his eyes blazing, dangerously intense.

Reaching into his inventory, the evil shadow-crafter slowly pulled out his iron sword.

"Ahhh . . . I mean . . . I mean, *your* Endermen are bringing the monsters here," Erebus stammered.

"That's what I thought," Herobrine replied as he slid his sword back into his inventory.

A group of lanky Endermen appeared nearby, each holding a pair of monsters in their long, clammy arms. After depositing the creatures on the rough-hewn floor, the dark beings teleported to the stream of water that fell from the ceiling of the cavern. The Endermen stood under the falling water, a look of bliss in their white eyes as their HP rejuvenated.

When Herobrine made the dark creatures, he'd poured every bit of hate and loathing he had for the villagers into them, but the Maker also gave them his overwhelming vanity and arrogance. The vanity made the creatures always want to clean themselves, and in cleansing their skin, they would replace any lost HP. The arrogance from Herobrine made the Endermen so confident in battle that they assumed no villager would ever dare hit them. As a result, they could not join the battle unless they were first attacked or challenged with a direct stare. Somehow, the villagers had learned of this, making the Endermen almost useless at the start of wars, but keeping them around still had its advantages. For example, they were very effective at transporting troops from place to place.

"Soon, my Maker, we'll have transported all of the scattered monsters across the Overworld to your zombie-towns," Erebus continued, his screechy voice echoing off the cold stone walls. "By nightfall, we'll have a vast army of angry creatures ready to serve their Maker."

"Excellent. Soon we'll be ready to move against that pathetic blacksmith and his cowardly followers," Herobrine sneered.

"Maker, I don't mean to question your plan, but I don't see any spiders here," Erebus said cautiously.

A cloud of purple teleportation particles began to dance about his skin, ready to carry the dark monster away in case his question infuriated

Herobrine. The Enderman had quickly realized that most questions did.

"Relax, Erebus," the dark virus replied. "The spiders are on another task, but they will join us soon. First, they have a target to eliminate. I have ordered Shaikulud to continue her hunt until she is successful."

"What does she pursue?" Erebus asked.

Herobrine smiled but said nothing, then turned and watched as more Endermen appeared, each with one or two monsters in their grasp. As soon as they deposited their cargo in the cavern, they disappeared, hunting for more zombies and skeletons.

"What of the survivors from the last battle with Smithy and the villagers?" Erebus asked.

"They're gathering at Dragon's Teeth," the Maker explained. "There are three to four dozen monsters waiting for us there. When the rest of the army is assembled, and we know where the blacksmith is located, we'll bring all the monsters together and finally crush our enemy."

"But how do you know where the villagers are hiding?"

"My ghasts seek the blacksmith from high overhead. When they find him, a few of the monsters will attack while one of them flies away and reports to their king, Malacoda."

Erebus growled at the sound of the ghast king.

"I do not trust this Malacoda," Erebus said. "He's overly arrogant and boasts of his successes before he has done anything. That ghast cannot be trusted."

"My, my, Erebus, are you a little jealous?" Herobrine said with a wry smile.

"It's not jealousy," the Enderman snapped. "I only seek to serve the Maker, but I question if this

Malacoda serves Herobrine, or merely himself? At the first sign of trouble, he floats high into the air as do the rest of his ghasts, rather than stay near the ground and fight. They're all cowards. That over-inflated gas-bag cannot be trusted. I could destroy him for you . . . if you wish."

"You will do nothing of the kind," Herobrine growled, his eyes glowing bright, causing the king of the Endermen to take a step back. "Malacoda is able to control the other ghasts, and that makes him valuable. As long as he follows my orders, the king of the ghasts will not be harmed. Is that understood?"

"Yes, Maker," Erebus replied in a meek voice.

"Very good, my Enderman king. For now, we wait as we gather more zombies, skeletons, ghasts, and newly-spawned Endermen. When we know of our enemy's location, I will loose my forces upon him and watch Smithy writhe in sorrow and despair before he is destroyed. But until that time, we wait and prepare."

The Maker looked at his ever-growing army, his eyes glowing a harsh white, then laughed a malicious laugh as he thought of all the ways he was going to torture the blacksmith, before finally destroying him.

CHAPTER 10

MEETING IN THE FOREST

They reached the edge of the savanna just after sunset. Gameknight knew they could have traveled faster, but he felt stealth and caution would serve them better than speed. As a result, they moved in small groups of three, one person guiding while a second watched the terrain around them, and a third monitored the sky. They ran from tree to tree, trying to stay under cover whenever possible, hoping to avoid detection from above.

Wilbur acted as their monster detector; his sensitive nose seemed to pick up the scent of monsters when they were far away, as he recently had with the spiders. So Gameknight stayed on one side of the little pink animal, with Weaver on the other as they ran from tree to tree. For now, the tiny pig detected nothing, but the User-that-is-not-a-user was certain that would not last long.

When they reached the oak forest that bordered the savanna, the warriors all breathed a sigh of relief. Now, instead of having to run across large stretches of open land to get to the next tree, they would be able to stay under the leafy canopy, which was much safer.

They moved quickly through the forest in that manner, sometimes sprinting, while other times walking to catch their breath. At first, Gameknight thought he'd have to slow down so the Oracle could keep up, but the old woman never seemed to get winded. She always stayed at Gameknight's side, the tall form of Treebrin and the squat Grassbrin next to her, the other light-crafters trailing behind.

"We need scouts out on our flanks," Gameknight said quietly. "We can't shout out to find Carver and the other villagers. It might attract some unwanted attention. Instead, we need to use our ears."

"I'll go to the left," one villager said.

"I'm on the right," another added.

The two NPCs moved off, their armor clanking ever so slightly. Gameknight watched as they disappeared into the darkness, then turned and continued northward.

"I'm going up ahead," Weaver said. "I'll be quiet and no one will know I'm there."

The young boy took off his iron armor and put on some black leather armor he had in his inventory. Against the background of the dark forest, he was so hard to see that he nearly disappeared.

"I'll come back if I see anything."

"Just be careful," Gameknight insisted.

If anything happens to him, it could change everything, he thought.

"Don't worry. That's a resourceful young man," the Oracle said at his side. "He'll be fine."

The User-that-is-not-a-user tried to smile, but all he could manage was a strained grimace.

They continued forward, eyes searching the skies as their ears scanned the forest. Just then, they heard a muffled, baby-like cry. Everyone stopped.

"Did you hear that?" Gameknight whispered.

Some of the NPCs nodded their boxy heads, scared looks on their faces. He glanced at the Oracle.

"Do you think that was a ghast?" the User-that-is-not-a-user asked.

"I can't be sure," the old woman replied.

She glanced at her light-crafters. Treebrin and Cactusbrin ran forward, followed by Grassbrin. Dirtbrin and the gray-skinned Stonebrin stayed at her side.

"They will offer us some defenses if needed," the Oracle said. "But I think we need to continue on."

"Agreed," Gameknight confirmed.

He drew his bow and notched an arrow, then began to walk again. Weaving around stout oak trees, Gameknight glanced through the tree branches, searching for anything floating in the sky.

Another soft, baby-like cry floated to them from ahead and to the right.

That could have been a ghast, the User-that-is-not-a-user thought. *Sometimes they sound like a cat and other times like a baby. I need to figure out some kind of defense if they decide to attack.*

Focusing on his surroundings, Gameknight tried to come up with a battle plan . . . but he had nothing. The stress of continually having to come up with one strategy after another was wearing on him; the responsibility for everyone's safety felt overwhelming at times.

Without any real idea coming to him, Gameknight continued forward, his eyes cast upward, peering through the leaves. Another cry floated through the forest, muffled, as if the source were trying to hide their location. Gripping his bow firmly, he moved directly toward the sound. He'd rather face a threat directly before him than let it sneak up behind him. Running faster, he dashed up the gentle hills that dotted the landscape, hoping to get a clear view of what lay ahead.

The cry called out again. Gameknight couldn't be sure, but he thought it came from the other side of the next hill.

"Come on," the User-that-is-not-a-user growled. "Now we sprint!"

He charged forward with an arrow drawn back, ready to fire. The sound of twenty villagers, all in iron armor, clanked through the forest as they ran. When they reached the top of the rise and descended downward, the group skidded to a stop. Standing before them was a worn and haggard group of villagers led by Carver. Weaver stood next to the stocky NPC with a baby villager in his young arms.

"Carver!" Gameknight exclaimed. He ran forward and embraced his friend. "I'm so glad you're alright."

"We're certainly glad to see you," Carver replied. "We found Weaver here, and he was leading us back to you."

Gameknight pointed to the infant NPC, then gave Carver a questioning glance.

"She was just born a few hours ago," the proud father explained as he stepped forward. "She's a milker. I'm sure one day she will be the best cow milker in the village."

"Ahh . . . Milky," Gameknight said with a smile.
"That's a great name," Carver said. "We'll call her Milky."

The stocky villager turned and glanced at Weaver, who was looking down at the child in his arms and making goofy faces, trying to keep her from crying again.

Suddenly, footsteps could be heard in the forest. Gameknight turned to face the potential threat, an arrow ready to fire. The Oracle moved to Gameknight's side and carefully pushed his bow to the ground.

"Friends," she said to the User-that-is-not-a-user.

The light-crafters emerged from the darkness with the scouts that had been checking their flanks. The two NPCs visibly relaxed when they saw the other villagers, and patted Treebrin and Grassbrin on the back. But they only waved to Cactusbrin, whose prickly skin was not very welcoming.

Carver stepped up to his side and spoke in a low voice.

"Our village . . . it was destroyed," the stocky NPC said.

"I know," Gameknight replied.

"How do you . . .?"

"It's difficult to explain," Gameknight interrupted. "When we are somewhere safe. . . ." He trailed off, then glanced at the faces of the villagers. "Where's your village's leader, Farmer?"

"He didn't make it," Carver replied. "Farmer was on the walls when they attacked. He was the first one to be hit by a fireball."

"I'm sorry," Gameknight replied.

"So who's in charge now?" Weaver asked as he handed the baby back to the parents.

"Well," Carver replied. "I guess . . ."

"You are, Carver," Gameknight snapped in a loud voice. "There is a village south of here in the savanna. We need to get your people there so they can rest."

A cry filled the air again.

"Weaver, can you try to keep that baby quiet again?" Gameknight said. "I'd rather no one knows we're out here."

"It wasn't Milky," Weaver said, pointing to the infant.

The baby was asleep in the father's arms.

"Then where did the cry come from?" Carver asked.

Gameknight glanced at Carver. They both had expressions of fear chiseled in their square faces.

"Everyone, get under a tree," the User-that-is-not-a-user said as he glanced skyward.

Moving under a large oak, the User-that-is-not-a-user peered through the branches. Stars still sparkled down at them, but some disappeared as dark rectangles floated across the sky: clouds.

Icicles of fear stabbed at him as Gameknight searched the heavens for their enemy. Around him were now maybe fifty villagers that needed protection, and it fell upon Gameknight999 to figure out how to keep them all safe.

I hate this responsibility, he thought. *Sometimes it's overwhelming, being the sole person they all look to for safety.*

He moved around the trunk of the tree and leaned out from under the foliage to get a better view of the sky. Just then, nine long tentacles descended down from a cloud. A feeling of dread washed over him.

"Ghasts," the User-that-is-not-a-user whispered just as a fireball streaked through the air, right at them.

CHAPTER 11

FOREST OF FLAMES

The fireball exploded just overhead.

Wilbur oinked, just as surprised by the blast as the villagers were.

"The ghast missed," Gameknight exclaimed. "Its attack hit the oak tree instead of making it to the ground."

"They won't make that mistake again," the Oracle said in her scratchy, ancient voice.

"Everyone move," the User-that-is-not-a-user said. "If you stand still, the monsters will certainly shoot at you. Everyone run. Head to the south."

The villagers ran as fast as they could to the south, trying to keep under the cover of the many trees that covered the landscape. Gameknight moved to the newborn infant's parents. He stayed near them in case a fireball came toward them, so it could be batted away. Wilbur, too, stayed near Milky, the tiny pig determined to protect her as well. Gameknight knew the baby was the ancestor of one of his friends from the future. Milky was related to Crafter, somehow, and he knew she had to be kept safe, as did all these villagers. But as a relative of his friend, she was especially important to him.

I'm not gonna let any ghast shoot a fireball at a baby, Gameknight thought, his courage pushing back the fear of responsibility. *Not on my watch!*

As they ran, more attacks rained down from overhead. Trees exploded, turning into huge, towering infernos as flames from the top slowly crept across the branches and spread to the neighboring oaks. Gameknight glanced over his shoulder at the forest fire that was now pursuing them. The sky behind them glowed an angry orange as sparks and embers leapt up into the air, only to settle down onto an innocent block of leaves and bring more flames to life. Fortunately, there were places throughout the forest where the trees were spaced apart; the fire would not be able to spread far. But the thinning of the trees caused other problems. The ghasts would now be able to see them easier.

Gameknight ran as he peered up into the sky, searching for the floating monstrosities. It was hard to flee and look over his shoulder at the same time. He found himself almost colliding into trees or other villagers.

"I don't like this," the User-that-is-not-a-user said to Weaver, who ran next to him. "The ghasts are just gonna continue this line of attack until they drive us out of the forest."

"What do you want to do?" the young boy asked.

"LOOK OUT!" Gameknight screamed as he shoved Weaver to the side.

A fireball exploded right where he'd been running. The hem of his smock was slightly singed, and thin tendrils of smoke began to snake up into the air.

"It's time we stop retreating and start attacking!" the User-that-is-not-a-user growled.

He dashed forward and whispered into the Oracle's ear. The old woman nodded, then motioned for her light-crafters to approach. As they conferred, Gameknight ran to the different groups of warriors and explained his plan. Once one group understood, he went to the next one, and then the next, until they were all ready.

The light-crafters ran ahead at incredible speeds, disappearing into the forest.

"Oracle, are we ready?" Gameknight asked.

"I think so," she replied.

"What are you doing?" Carver asked.

"We're planning a little surprise for the ghasts," the User-that-is-not-a-user said. "Just keep your people running south, and don't stop until you hear me shout."

"Got it," he replied, then took Milky in his big hands to give the father a chance to rest his arms.

Ahead, Gameknight saw the light-crafters Treebrin, Grassbrin, and Cactusbrin standing near a bunch of saplings. Atop each young tree was a block of dirt. He wasn't really sure how they did that, and didn't care, as long as it worked.

"Get on the blocks," Gameknight said.

Another fireball exploded behind them as the angry cat-like cries from the ghasts filled the air.

The archers all stood on top of a sapling with their bows notched. They turned and faced the approaching monsters, fear painted on every blocky face. Gameknight mounted his plant and waited. Suddenly, Treebrin's arms began to shine a deep, forest green. When the glow reached his elbows, the lanky light-crafter plunged them into the ground. Instantly, the trees sprouted upward, forming a towering wall of full-grown spruce trees, an archer perched standing precariously on each.

"FIRE!" Gameknight shouted.

A wave of arrows flew through the air, streaking toward the pristine white monsters that approached. Gameknight saw there were five of them, all spread out in a line. Firing his arrow, he drew and fired again and again. They all knew if they didn't destroy the ghasts right away, then they were sitting ducks.

Cries of pain came from the monsters as their barbed projectiles found their targets. One of the monsters howled a cat-like yowl, then turned sideways as its HP was finally exhausted. A ball of fire streaked to the tree to his left. The villager saw the burning sphere of death approaching and had no choice but to jump. Hopefully, he would land in the leaves of an oak tree, and would not take all that fall damage. If he hit the ground, the NPC would likely not survive.

Gameknight fired a trio of arrows at the monster, striking it with the first two and silencing its cries. He then turned and fired on another ghast as other archers did the same. A wave of arrows descended on the doomed creature, destroying it before it could launch another fireball.

"YEAH!" shouted the archers as they admired the clear sky.

Gameknight looked at the line of trees. Four of the ten newly grown trees were consumed with flames. It wasn't clear whether the warriors had escaped the infernos or not. But then he noticed one of the burning trees had a column of water falling from a block of leaves; at least one of them had.

Pulling out his own bucket of water that he'd brought with him from the village, he poured it over the edge of the treetop. After a few seconds, he jumped into the watery flow and rode it safely to the ground. As he descended, Gameknight saw the devastation to the forest behind them. Huge sections of the forest were burning, casting a glow on the surroundings that was partially obscured by the billowing smoke climbing into the air.

"We need to put the fire out," one of the villagers said as he stepped out of the falling water.

"No, it will burn itself out soon enough," Gameknight said. "Did anyone see how many ghasts were attacking us? We need to know if we destroyed them all or not."

"Why are you so worried?" Carver asked. "They're gone now."

"If any of them managed to escape," the User-that-is-not-a-user explained, "they'll go straight back to Herobrine and tell him where we are. We need to get out of here, fast."

"I think there were only five of them," one of the woodcutters said.

"But I think there were some more monsters farther back," a farmer added. "I saw something glowing in the sky."

"Yeah, me too," a familiar voice said.

Gameknight scanned the crowd until he found the owner of the voice.

"Fisher, you're alright!" the User-that-is-not-a-user exclaimed.

"Yep, but just barely, Smithy," the lanky boy explained. "I never made it to the desert village. The ghast caught me out in the open. If it weren't for that desert well, I wouldn't be here right now."

"We found him after we evacuated our village," Carver explained. "He was coming toward us while we were leaving."

"Well, I'm glad you're alright," Gameknight said and patted the boy on the back. "But back to the point: we don't know for sure if any of the ghasts escaped. They knew we were heading to the south, so we need to do something else, or they'll be waiting for us."

"You could head to the southwest, to the mega taiga biome," an old NPC said. Gameknight instantly recognized him as Mapper from Carver's village. "There's a village just on the outskirts of the biome. We could head for that village, then veer to the southeast and reach your village."

"I like that plan," Gameknight commended. "We'll get back to our village a little later, but we'll hopefully avoid meeting any more ghasts. I think we can all agree that would be best."

He glanced over his shoulder and saw a pile of armor, weapons, and food floating off the ground, the contents of a deceased villager's inventory, someone who'd been destroyed by the fiery monsters. Slowly, Gameknight raised his hand into the air, fingers spread wide in the salute for the dead. The other villagers raised their hands as well.

"We'll get back to the village and figure out how to stop Herobrine," Gameknight growled as anger began to bubble up from within his soul. "The sacrifice our friends and family members have made here in these woods will not be forgotten." He squeezed his hand into a fist, clenching it tighter and tighter as he squeezed out the guilt he felt over the loss of these villagers. The NPCs around him drew their hands into fists, rage boiling in their eyes. When his knuckles began to pop, he released his fist and lowered his outstretched arm.

"Let's get going," Carver said. "The sooner we are in a village, the happier I'll be."

"Agreed," Gameknight replied. "But first, where is Fisher?"

"Here," the skinny NPC replied.

"I have another task for you," the User-that-is-not-a-user said.

He moved close to the young villager and whispered in his ear, the boy nodding his head in return.

"Weaver, give Fisher your black armor," Gameknight instructed.

He pulled out the dark armor and handed it over, then donned a set of iron.

Fisher put the dark leather coating on and nearly disappeared in the dark forest.

"Now go," Gameknight said.

The lanky youth gave the blacksmith a smile, then took off running to the south.

"Where is he going?" Carver asked.

"He'll tell Fencer and the others where we are heading," Gameknight explained. "I fear we'll be needing their swords before this is over."

Glancing at the moon, he found his bearings and started through the forest toward the mega taiga biome that lay hidden behind the horizon. The rest of the villagers followed in silence, their eyes cast both into the darkness of the forest, but also up at the clear sky above.

None of them noticed the cluster of angry red dots that peered down at them from atop the trees. Quietly, one of them slowly rose from behind a block of leaves, then turned toward another of its kind.

"I will return to the Maker and tell him we have found the enemy," the spider said quietly.

"And I will go to the queen," another said.

"Yessss, Sssshaitar, inform the queen while we continue to follow them," a third spider said. There were another two more still hiding in the leaves, watching the villagers. "Our queen, Sssshaikulud, will be able to find ussss. We will sssstay near the NPCssss but out of sssssight."

"Good," the monster said.

The spider turned and headed northeast, back toward Herobrine and his growing monster army, while Shaitar headed toward the jungle biome that sat off to the northwest. As the two dark monsters scurried away, the remaining three creatures moved noiselessly across the treetops, always keeping the fleeing army just in sight, their eyes glowing bright red with evil thoughts of destruction.

CHAPTER 12

SPIDERS

Shaikulud hung from the ceiling of the large cavern, an impossibly thin strand of silk connecting her to the stone overhead. She gazed about the shadowy chamber, her eight purple eyes casting spots of lavender light on the stone walls. Blocks of spider web sat in the corners and along the floors and ceiling, giving the cave an ancient feeling, even though the monsters had just recently taken over this space.

Within many of the delicate white webs sat a black egg, red spots spattered across its surface. Some rocked ever so gently, while other eggs remained still. Shaikulud noticed many of the eggs cracked open, with small spiders struggling to work their way free from the eggshell and web. But no one helped them. This was their first test in life, and if they were not strong enough to free themselves, then they perished; it was the spider way.

Spiders smaller than Shaikulud, and dark-blue in color, scurried through the chamber, inspecting each egg and making sure the webs were secure. They were the Brothers, the cave spiders. It was their job to tend the cave and care for the hatchlings. There were at least twenty of the smaller creatures moving all throughout the cavern, checking all of their charges with care. Some were coming into the chamber with large clumps of green moss to feed the newborns. It had been pulled off mossy cobblestone blocks and was the favorite food of a newborn spider, nourishing their young bodies to full health quickly so they could serve the queen as soon as possible.

"Thissss crop of hatchlingssss will be large," the queen said to herself.

Her eyes grew bright with evil thoughts of the destruction these new spiders would bring down upon the villagers. She imagined them as a dark wave flowing across the Overworld, destroying village after village.

Suddenly, a clicking sound filled the air as a fuzzy black spider entered the chamber. Shaikulud instantly grew angry and lowered herself to the ground, her mandibles snapping together, creating an angry clatter. All spiders knew the hatchery was only for the Brothers, and that the larger black spiders, the Sisters, could not enter.

She charged toward her offending subject, the razor-sharp curved claws at the end of each leg clicking on the dusty stone floor. As she neared, the dark spider lowered her head to the floor and spoke quickly.

"The enemy hassss been found," the giant spider said, a scared tremor in the monster's voice.

"What?" Shaikulud said. "You found the blacksssssmith?"

"Yessss, my queen," the sister replied.

Shaikulud reached out with one clawed arm. The dark spider cringed, expecting a deadly strike to land at any moment. But instead, the spider queen gently patted the fuzzy creature on the head.

"You have done well, Ssssisssster," she said to her subject. "Issss sssshe with him?"

"Yessss my queen," the spider replied.

"Excellent," the queen of the spiders said. "Sssshow me their location."

The spider nodded, then turned and headed out of the hatching chamber, Shaikulud following close behind. They passed many of their sisters in the passages, the dark creatures merging in with the darkness and becoming almost invisible, except for their eyes, which all glowed bright red, like angry little embers. The ones they passed quickly filed behind their queen. They could feel there was something happening, something important, and all of the spiders wanted to serve their queen to the best of their abilities.

After racing along the curving tunnel to the surface, the spider climbed the nearest junglewood tree and moved to the peak of the leafy giant. Atop the green canopy, Shaikulud found other spiders laying on the treetops, waiting for the sun that was just rising above the eastern horizon. A splash of red appeared across the sky. It was bright and deep, like a spider's eyes. Slowly, the crimson line grew upward as the sun rose, fading to a bright orange. The stars disappeared with the unrelenting advance of the sun's radiant square face, the sky slowly changing to the deep blue hue of day.

More spiders emerged from the underground tunnels and moved to the top of the jungle, hoping to catch the first rays of the morning sun. This jungle was the location Shaikulud had chosen for their hatchery. With the thick forest and bushes across the ground, and the cave entrance nearly impossible to find, it made the perfect place for them to call home.

The spider queen turned and faced her sister.

"Where wassss the blacksssssmith found?" she asked.

The spider pointed her curved claw to the south.

"The enemy wasssss found in that direction," the sister reported. "He wassss with many villagerssss, some of them hungry and tired."

"That meanssss they'll need to find a village ssssoon," Shaikulud said.

"There are ssssssissssterssss following them," the spider reminded her queen.

Shaikulud nodded, then closed her eight purple eyes. Reaching out with the psychic powers given to her by Herobrine during her making, she felt for the spiders across the great expanse of the Overworld. Instantly, she could sense their presence in the distance. With a careful and light touch, the spider queen probed the minds of her subjects.

"Ahhh . . . I ssssee they are following them into a biome with extremely large treessss," the queen said. She glanced around at the monsters that stood nearby. "We will move ssssouth and help our ssssisssssters with the blacksssssmith and the old woman." Shaikulud turned to the monster that brought her the news. "What issss your name, child?"

"I am called Ssssshaitar," the spider said.

"Well done, Ssssshaitar," the queen commended. "Now go to Herobrine and tell him of thissss newsssss. My sssspider army will catch them sss-soon enough."

Shaitar moved quickly across the treetops toward the rising sun and Dragon's Teeth. Likely the other spider from their party was heading toward Herobrine as well, but that did not matter. That spider could be caught by villagers or wounded in a fall and never make it to the Maker. Shaitar would also travel across the land to give this news to Herobrine, as the queen had ordered.

The spider queen watched the creature scurry away, then charged to the south. As she streaked across the green leafy carpet, her subjects dutifully followed. They flowed up out of the jungle greenery and spread across the treetops. It was as if a black wave of claws and glowing eyes were flooding over the land as more and more fuzzy monsters joined the pursuit.

Shaikulud closed most of her eyes and imagined what she would do to the old woman when she found her. The Oracle, she called herself . . . the name made the spider queen's eyes burn bright with hatred. That hag had destroyed hundreds of her sisters with her filthy light-crafters. The spider queen was going to laugh as her sisters destroyed those pathetic crafters, then they would turn their claws toward the Oracle; that was when the real fun would begin.

CHAPTER 13
MEGA TAIGA

They reached the end of the oak forest by sunrise. Beyond the cluster of trees stood the alien and mystical ice spikes biome. Tall spires of glacial blue ice stretched up into the sky like frozen spears thrown upward from the ground, trying to impale the heavens.

"Let's rest for a bit," Gameknight said.

Many of the NPCs from Carver's village collapsed to the ground and were instantly asleep. Those who had food distributed it to anyone in need, but they soon realized they were quickly running out, so Gameknight sent some of the warriors out into the forest with axes. They collected wood and trimmed many of the leaves back, hoping to find the elusive red apples hidden in the leafy canopy.

Meanwhile, Gameknight moved to Carver's side, Mapper standing nearby.

"Mapper, how much farther is this mega taiga village?" Gameknight asked.

"Well, it's not really in the taiga, but right next to it," the old NPC explained. "It should be on the other side of the ice spikes."

"We need to hurry up and find it. I don't like being out in the open during the day." Gameknight glanced to the east. The horizon was already painted with reds and oranges as the dark starry sky slowly retreated from the advancing sun. "We need a safe place for everyone to rest."

"Don't worry, Smithy. We'll find the village," Carver said. "I have faith Mapper knows where we are going. He'll get us there."

Suddenly, someone was shouting at them from the ice spikes. Turning, Gameknight saw a figure at the top of one of the frozen spires, a series of icy steps wrapping around the blue column. The User-that-is-not-a-user ran to see who it was and what it was they were saying. As he neared, he realized it was Weaver at the top of the translucent pillar.

"What are you doing up there?" Gameknight shouted.

"Smithy, I can see the mega taiga forest from here," the young boy said in a loud voice.

The NPC carefully used the steps of snow and ice he'd placed and descended from on high. When he reached the ground, he smiled at Gameknight999.

"I know you were worried about where we were going, so I went up and checked everything out," Weaver explained. "Mapper here is dead on; we're heading straight for a forest of gigantic trees."

"Excellent," Gameknight said, "but next time, tell me what you're doing. That climb was far too dangerous. If you had fallen, you might have. . . ." He couldn't finish the sentence.

How do I keep him safe when he never listens to me? Gameknight thought. *Maybe I'm not a strong enough leader to protect him.*

He glanced at Carver. The stocky NPC was a natural leader. Villagers flocked to stand at his side now that he'd become comfortable with who he really was. They called him the "Carver of monsters," and his skill with his shining axe was respected by everyone. But it wasn't just his physical strength they looked up to; it was his moral strength, and his concern for others, and his positive outlook on life, and. . . . There were a hundred reasons why they should look up to the stocky NPC, but the only reason Gameknight could think of that the villagers would look up to him was his two swords. He was still pretending to be someone else, Smithy, and the longer the ruse went on, the harder it was to come clean to everyone and tell the truth. It weighed heavily on him; the User-that-is-not-a-user felt as if he were a lie.

"Sorry I worried you," Weaver said, snapping Gameknight back to the present. "I'll let you know in advance next time I do something dangerous."

The boy smiled at his idol.

"That's not what I mean," the User-that-is-not-a-user said.

Both Weaver and Carver laughed.

"Let's get everyone moving," Carver said.

The stocky NPC gathered the villagers. They rose wearily and continued the march to the west, through the icy landscape. Their breath turned to fog in the air as the chill began to settle into their bones, their feet crunching as they made their way through the snow and ice. It was the only sound in the biome; there was a strange absence of animals, making the frosty terrain seem more barren than even the harshest of deserts. But true to Weaver's word, they eventually began to see the tops of massive spruce trees peeking up from behind snow-covered hills.

When they reached the edge of the ice spikes biome, they finally saw their destination: a village. Surprisingly, it was a desert village, not one in the mega taiga forest. A narrow strip of desert extended between the ice spikes and mega taiga biomes. The village sat on the sliver of sand and cactus, and the sandstone houses in it looked very out of place, being so close to the ice spikes and tall spruce trees.

"There it is!" Weaver exclaimed.

"Yeah, but where are all the people?" Gameknight asked.

The desert village looked completely empty.

"Let's go down and find out," Carver said, his booming voice making the icy spires nearby reverberate.

The tired and haggard army moved down the snowy hill and entered the desert. The air went from chilly and crisp to dry and dusty in an instant. The heat slammed into them like a hammer; it was a shockingly sudden change. Now, with sweat running down their faces and necks, they moved to the center of the clustered buildings and gathered around the central well.

"I see footsteps going toward the forest," Mapper said, pointing.

Gameknight glanced to the sand, but saw nothing. Regardless, Mapper took off toward the towering trees, following the subtle tracks. In seconds, they had left the desert and moved into the mega taiga. The temperature dropped again, providing them all a bit of relief from the oppressive heat, the dry and dusty smell giving way to one thick with the wood and leaves and grass.

Huge trees stretched up to the sky, taller than any others found in Minecraft. They were two blocks wide instead of just one like all the other oaks and birches and pines. Broad, leafy ferns dotted the ground, stretching out to catch any rays of sun that managed to make it all the way to the forest floor. A strange brownish soil, called podzol, covered the ground. It had the texture of gravel, with lots of specks decorating its face, but the colors were made of warm oranges, dark chocolate browns, and subtle shades of green. Dotting the landscape were clusters of mossy cobblestone. It was the only place you could find these blocks on the surface of the Overworld. Brown mushrooms covered the few shady patches of grass that were struggling to grow. They didn't last long. Carver had villagers harvest the mushrooms to be used for stew. The whole scene—the towering trees, the colorful podzol, mushrooms, and green rocky stone—was magnificent.

In Gameknight's timeline, in the present, they would have likely heard the howls of wolves; mega taigas were a favorite biome of the furry creatures. But in this time, the distant past, no howls could be heard. It would have made his friend, Herder, very sad, the User-that-is-not-a-user thought.

Stepping up to one of the massive spruce trees, Gameknight peered up along its trunk. He expected to see all the way to the leaf-covered limbs, but instead he found there were blocks of wood placed sporadically around their trunks for some reason. Maybe they were severed tree limbs? But that didn't make sense; the limbs were all near the top of the trees. Something wasn't right here.

Suddenly, the rustling of leaves overhead drew Gameknight's attention. Slowly he pulled out his bow and looked upward nonchalantly. Far above him, he could see boxy feet pressing against the thick, leafy blocks that stretched out from the gigantic trees.

"'Something's up in the trees," Gameknight whispered.

Slowly, he moved through the forest, fitting an arrow to his bow and drawing it back ever so quietly. The bow creaked under the strain.

"I wouldn't do that," a soft voice said from high above him.

Gameknight stopped and glanced toward the sound, the rest of the villagers also freezing in place. Before any of them could draw a weapon, villagers emerged from the leaves overhead, some of them moving down the thick tree trunks, jumping down the strategically placed blocks along the outside of the giants, while others cut away leaves with shears and stared straight down on them, arrows notched and drawn.

"I think all of you should put your weapons down before someone gets hurt," one of the NPCs in the trees said.

A woman in a light-brown smock jumped to a lower block of wood on the side of a tall spruce. She held a bow with the arrow drawn and pointed at Gameknight999. He could tell by the way the NPC held that bow that she knew how to shoot.

"It's okay," a scratchy voice said.

Gameknight glanced to the side and found the Oracle standing next to him. She reached out with her wrinkled hand and slowly pushed his bow down to the ground.

"They are friends," she added. "You do not need your weapon here, child."

The User-that-is-not-a-user nodded, then put away his bow. He then motioned the other villagers to do the same.

"We are friends," Gameknight complained. "Why would you aim your bows at us?"

"These are strange days, with monsters moving all across the land in broad daylight and tons of spiders scurrying about," the woman said. "We're only being cautious." She relaxed the tension on the bowstring, then put away her weapon. "It's okay, everyone. Come on down."

Gracefully, the woman jumped down the blocks that were placed around the trunk of the massive tree. With every leap, the smallest puff of white came from her clothing . . . strange. But then he figured it out; she was a baker.

Baker led the way to the ground, villagers descending behind her from multiple trees. They all moved with a catlike grace, as if they'd been using these steps to the treetops all their lives. When the NPCs made it to the ground, they spread out in a defensive formation in case there were any monsters nearby. Gameknight appreciated their efficiency.

Once the area was secure, Baker approached. Instantly, he was shocked by her bright blue eyes; they reminded him of Weaver, and his friend in the future, Crafter. And then Gameknight remembered his friend telling him something about a distant relative; maybe her name was Baker, but he couldn't be sure. Crafter told so many stories about his ancestors that it was hard to keep them all straight in his head.

"What is it you need here?" she asked.

"We have villagers in need of healing," Gameknight explained. "Their desert village was destroyed by ghasts and some are wounded. They need food and a place to sleep for a while."

"Of course. Quickly, bring them to our village."

Baker led them through the forest and onto the narrow slice of desert. As they passed from the brown, mushroom-covered soil to the sandy ground, the heat of the desert slammed into them again. He knew it was coming, but going from cool to hot was still quite a shock.

Square beads of sweat ran down his forehead and tumbled into his eyes as he ran into the pale-yellow village. There was no wall protecting the NPCs who lived here, nor was there any watchtower. After moving to the well, he turned to look back at the tall spruces. Several villagers could be seen atop the trees, scanning the terrain. He felt better knowing they were keeping watch; he was sure they were safe . . . for now.

Baker approached from one of the nearby houses, her smock covered with a light coating of flour. She slapped at her shoulders and chest, creating a subtle white cloud that slowly settled to the ground.

"Tell me what happened to these villagers," Baker said. "I saw some that were badly burned."

"As I told you, the ghasts attacked their village and leveled it to the ground," Gameknight explained. "An evil virus named Herobrine has sworn to destroy all the NPCs across the Overworld, so that the monsters can roam free. No doubt he'll be on your doorstep, eventually, with a monster army at his back."

"I've seen the ghasts," Baker said. "A group of three floated by last night. They looked kinda strange, as if they were suddenly angry at something. We felt it best to hide in the trees."

"So they didn't see you?" Gameknight asked.

"Monsters see us only when we let them," Baker said with a hint of pride.

"That's good," he replied with a nod. "I fear we'll need all of you to help, once we figure out what Herobrine's game is. I'm sure he's going to—"

Suddenly, an arrow struck the ground near Baker's feet. She turned and looked up quickly at one of the tall spruce trees. A village could be seen standing with his bow held out to the side, a handful of arrows in the other pointing straight up into the air.

"Spiders," Baker said, interpreting the signal.

"They were probably sent here by Herobrine," Gameknight said. "You can be sure they know we're here, and a monster army is on its way."

"We can fight them off," Baker boasted. "We've done it before. They can't touch us when we're up in our trees."

"They can if there are ghasts and spiders with them, and there will be, you can be sure of that."

"Then what do you expect us to do?" Baker asked.

"We have to leave here and head to a place that's more defensible," Gameknight explained. "There aren't enough forces here to stand up against Herobrine. I'm sure he's built his army back up by now. That evil virus will hit us with everything he has."

"Then we need to go get more troops."

"That would be great, of course," the User-that-is-not-a-user said. "You have somewhere in mind?"

"I know of a place in the savanna, southwest of here," Baker said. "It's the biggest village around, and they have defenses that could keep even the mightiest of armies back."

"We must move fast then. If Herobrine catches us out in the open, we'll be in serious trouble." Gameknight motioned to Carver who came to his side. "They spotted spiders watching us. You can be sure Herobrine knows where we are. We can't stay here and rest."

The stocky NPC nodded, then sighed. He was clearly exhausted, but as soon as he turned to face his villagers, he stood straight and tall, making it seem as if he could take on the world if necessary. His example inspired the others, making them all stand tall as well and push their fatigue aside for a little while longer.

He's a real *leader,* Gameknight thought with a bit of jealousy.

Quickly, the villagers gathered around the well to hear the plan, then moved out of the desert and into the mega taiga, traveling to the west for an hour before curving to the southwest, toward the distant savanna. But as they walked, Gameknight could feel the burning red eyes of the spiders watching and waiting, and he knew Herobrine's army was likely closing the distance.

CHAPTER 14

ENEMY REVEALED

The spider struggled through the desert sands, her HP dangerously low. She'd been running the entire day, starting from where they had seen the blacksmith and his rabble, and was heading toward the distant Dragon's Teeth, where the Maker would be waiting. But her health was continuing to drop; the rays of the sun doing little to replenish the energy she was consuming. Now, with the sun slowly setting behind the horizon, there was little hope of receiving any more HP from the glowing solar face. Hopefully, there would be some green moss nearby when she reached her final destination. If there wasn't, then it was likely she wouldn't survive the night. But it didn't matter; the spider was serving her queen, and there was nothing more important than that.

Pausing for a moment, the fuzzy monster collapsed to the ground to catch her breath. The four rocky spires were now easily visible beyond the next sand dune. The Maker would be there. Once she told him of the blacksmith's whereabouts, then her task would be complete and she could disappear into oblivion in peace, having served her queen to the end.

Standing on eight shaky legs, the dark creature picked herself back up and labored up the sand dune before tumbling down the other side, landing on hard stone. She'd moved out of the desert and into the extreme hills biome; at least that helped with the heat.

She stood and found one of her legs didn't work very well.

"I musssst have injured it when I fell," she said to herself.

Ahead, the spider could hear the sorrowful moans of zombies and the clattering of skeletons; she was almost there. Gathering all of her strength, the monster scurried across the rocky ground, pulling her one useless leg as she struggled to move. The claw on the injured appendage dragged across the ground, making a loud scraping sound that echoed off the stone cliffs nearby. She moved faster, trying to reach her goal before her HP ran out.

Suddenly, a tall, dark-red Enderman appeared before her. He reached down and picked up her frail body. A tingling sensation began to cover her skin as a cloud of purple particles filled her vision. For the briefest instant, she was able to see rocky cliffs and bright lava spilling down a steep stone spire, and a dark figure staring at her. The two images overlapped on each other; it was confusing. The spider wasn't sure where she was, and had the feeling of being at two places at once. Then, in a flash, she materialized before her Maker, Herobrine.

"Maker, he hassss been found," the spider said with a weak voice.

She could feel her health failing, she had to speak quickly.

"The blackssssmith."

"You found the blacksmith?" Herobrine asked, his eyes glowing bright.

The spider nodded her head. She was beginning to feel faint.

"He issss with a group of villagerssss to the ssss-south . . . wesssst," The spider was struggling to stay conscious. "Three ssssisssstersssss follow him. The queen issss being informed."

"This is excellent," Herobrine said, turning away from the fuzzy monster. "This means Shaikulud will be pursuing them soon, if she is not already . . . perfect!"

"What do you want to do with this spider?" Erebus asked. "She does not have long to live."

"I don't care. Do what you want with her," the Maker replied. "She has delivered her message and is no longer of any use to me."

"Very well," Erebus said, then disappeared. In seconds, he reappeared. "I left the spider in a dungeon. She'll be able to eat the moss off the stone walls and survive."

"Why do you think I care what happens to that spider?" Herobrine growled. "It's only one spider; I have hundreds of them!"

"Yes, Maker," the king of the Endermen replied.

"Erebus, it's time to assemble the army," the evil virus said. "Send some Endermen to find Shaikulud and her spider army."

Erebus glanced at three Endermen and pointed with a dark fist. They nodded and disappeared in a cloud of lavender mist in search of the spider queen.

"Send the rest of your Endermen to collect my monster army," Herobrine ordered. "Have them congregate in the chamber below us. When we learn of the spiders' location, we'll teleport my monsters to them."

"Will we attack the blacksmith when we find him?" Erebus asked, his eyes glowing red with evil excitement.

"No."

"No?" the Enderman king asked, confused.

"No. Instead, we'll push him across the Overworld to a place of our choosing. The foolish villager will think that the danger lies with my army, but we'll only be herding the NPCs to a place where my ghasts will destroy them. The idiotic fools will be looking to the ground, when they should have been keeping their eyes to the sky." He laughed an evil, malicious laugh, his eyes glowing like blazing suns.

"As long as we keep Smithy's attention focused on us, then we can drive him toward their doom. And in that moment, when nearly all of the villagers in his army are destroyed by my ghasts, you, Erebus, king of the Endermen, will teleport with me so you can watch me destroy the blacksmith with my own hands. Once he's gone, there will be nothing to bring the villagers together, for he's the only real leader amongst the NPCs. With his destruction, the rest of the villages will fall one after the other, for they are all cowards."

"That is a fantastic plan," Erebus said.

"Of course it is, fool!" Herobrine snapped. "Now go and bring me my monsters. I grow impatient standing here when my enemy is out there, waiting to be destroyed."

The king of the Endermen nodded, then disappeared in a cloud of purple mist. Herobrine closed his eyes, then teleported to the top of Dragon's Teeth, standing atop the tallest of the rocky spires. The sky to the west had turned a blood-red as the sun nestled behind the distant mountains and trees. That was his favorite moment, when the sky looked as if it had been stained in battle, but it only lasted for just a second. In no time, the sky had already changed to a dark crimson, then to black as the stars began to shine down on him.

Around him, sparkling orange clouds oozed from the stone peak and spread out in all directions, seeking the pristine white clouds that held the all-important ghasts within their misty rectangles.

"Soon, my infected clouds will cover all of Minecraft," Herobrine cackled. "With my massive army below and my ghasts above, nothing will be able to stand against me, not even the famous Smithy of the Two-swords. Soon, all of Minecraft will be mine."

He then laughed a vile, hate-filled laugh that made the very fabric of the Overworld cringe in fear.

CHAPTER 15

THE TRAP IS SPRUNG

The army ran all through the night and into the morning, trying to distance themselves from the spiders in hot pursuit. Gameknight knew they couldn't sprint the whole distance to the savanna village; some of Carver's NPCs were still weak from their battle with the ghasts that destroyed their village. So they shifted from sprinting to running, then to walking. They moved as fast as they could, and sometimes the weaker ones were scooped up and carried by the stronger.

It started to rain just before sunrise. Many of the villagers grumbled about getting wet, but rain was also a blessing in disguise; it meant they were more difficult to see. Even still, Gameknight hated the rain, for it meant clouds overhead. As they moved across the Overworld, the User-that-is-not-a-user kept his eyes on the dark storm clouds above them, watching for the telltale tentacles that would dangle below the misty rectangles right before an attack. Fortunately, the rain clouds overhead were devoid of ghasts.

For some reason, Wilbur seemed to like the downpour. The little pig jumped into small puddles and rolled through muddy creeks, trying to get as dirty as possible. It was a great distraction for the NPCs; they all smiled as they watched the simple joy on the animal's face. Unfortunately, the rain only lasted a few hours, and eventually the sun peeked up over the eastern horizon and began repainting the heavens overhead.

"We're making good time," the Oracle said. She'd been keeping to Gameknight's side throughout the evening, with her light-crafters always nearby.

"I see the village!" one of the scouts said, right on cue.

It was one of Baker's villagers. They'd been sent up ahead and told to climb one of the birch trees to look for their destination. Gameknight sprinted forward and found a tall one. Placing blocks of dirt under his feet, he built steps that would give him access to the treetops. Once he was on the leafy canopy, he looked in the direction the scout pointed . . . south.

In the distance, he could just barely see structures peeking through the haze of Minecraft. The next biome was savanna, just as predicted, and the village was there waiting for them. If he squinted his eyes and blocked the sunlight from hitting his face, he could just barely make the edges of wooden buildings, but everything else was too far away to see.

"I see it, too," Gameknight exclaimed. "Let's head south and get to that village."

But as the User-that-is-not-a-user climbed down from the trees, a chill spread over his body. The faint moaning of zombies could be heard in the direction of the village. And then came the chuckles of Endermen, causing tiny square goose bumps to form on the User-that-is-not-a-user's arms and neck.

Quickly, he ran back up to the treetops, then gasped in shock at what he saw. Monsters were appearing between his army and the savanna village, Endermen teleporting them into position, disappearing in a cloud of purple mist, only to reappear again with more snarling creatures in tow. As he watched, hundreds of monsters materialized, then stood next to each other—zombies, skeletons, and Endermen forming a lethal picket fence, blocking the villagers from the salvation of the village.

Cold beads of sweat formed on his brow as every nerve felt electrified with fear. Gameknight stared in disbelief at the assembly of monsters. Slowly, he descended from the treetops. By now, everyone in the army could hear the monsters in the distance.

"What is it?" Carver asked.

"Monsters," Gameknight replied.

"You think?" Baker added sarcastically.

"They've blocked us off from the savanna village," Gameknight explained, shaking his head. "If we head south, it would mean a direct battle with them. And with their numbers, I don't think we can win that conflict."

"Maybe we can go back and sneak around them?" Weaver suggested.

Just as Gameknight was about to answer, a clicking sound percolated through the forest from behind them. It was as if a million crickets were out there amongst the trees, chirping away with their angry song. He could tell from the volume that the monsters weren't close, but there were a lot of them, and they were probably coming fast.

Everyone heard the spiders and turned to face Gameknight999, expecting their leader, Smithy, to say or do something that would make everything okay. But he had nothing to say; there were two armies closing in on them and they were totally exposed, with no village walls to hide behind.

To make matters much, much worse, feline cries then drifted in from the north.

"Ghosts," Gameknight moaned. "What next . . . the ender dragon?"

"There's a dragon?!" Weaver exclaimed, his eyes wide with fear.

"No, there's no dragon. Just lots of monsters," the User-that-is-not-a-user quickly replied.

Another ghost screeched from the north. Anxious eyes glanced in the direction of the sound; none of them wanted to face the ghosts again, especially out in the open.

"It seems our choice has been made for us," Gameknight said. "The only direction we can go is west."

"Then let's get moving," Carver said in a loud, commanding voice. "Archers to the outside of the formation, elderly to the center. If anyone needs help running, let someone know and you'll be carried. LET'S GO!"

The army, buoyed by Carver's confidence, started running to the west. They emerged from the birch forest and began making their way across the savanna, the hot, dry air like a furnace. But this time, no one complained; desert air, no matter how uncomfortable it was, was always preferred to claws and fangs.

Acacia trees, each bent and twisted into a different shape, dotted the landscape. They were the only things visible around them, but as they ran over the large rolling hills, Gameknight became nervous.

We're easy to see on the hilltops, he thought. *We need to be more careful.*

Motioning to the big NPC, he had Carver lead the army *around* the hills instead of over, in hopes that the monsters would lose track of where they were.

But suddenly, spoiling their plans, a group of six spiders jumped out from a hole in the ground nearby, their black bodies scurrying rapidly over the savanna hill. They charged at the villagers, mandibles clicking together wildly, their eyes glowing bright red. Without thinking, Gameknight did the only thing he could think to do: drew his two swords and attacked.

Sprinting to the lead spider, he leapt high into the air, then landed right on top of the beast, smashing it with his swords. The monster squealed in pain and tried to knock him off, but Gameknight kept attacking until the spider disappeared with a *pop.*

There were only five of them left. Turning to the next one, he slashed at it as he ran past, then shot through their formation and attacked from the rear. By now, Carver and the other swordsmen had formed a line of armor and were pushing forward. The spider claws scratched at the metallic plating, causing damage, but as they focused on the warriors before them, Gameknight attacked from the rear. He slashed and poked with his swords, tearing at their HP as he sped by. Not bothering to stand and fight them one at a time, the User-that-is-not-a-user ran by and did small amounts of damage with each pass, just like in his dad's favorite game, Wing Commander. Hit and run, that's what he did, zipping past the fuzzy monsters with his swords spinning like two razor-sharp tornados. By the time the monsters reached Carver and his warriors, they had little HP left and were quickly destroyed.

"SMITHY!" the warriors chanted as he stepped through the battlefield, glowing balls of XP flowing into his feet.

Many of the NPCs had stopped during the attack. Those from Baker's village were shocked at the ferocity of Gameknight's fighting, not to mention the whole two-sword thing.

"They should have known not to mess with Smithy of the Two-swords," Weaver said, pride filling his voice.

Wilbur oinked as more villagers cheered, their shouts drowning out the clicking of the massive spider army still moving through the forest.

"SMITHY!" they shouted again.

"That doesn't matter right now," Gameknight said. "We can't stop . . . we have to keep going. That horde of spiders back there will not be so easily overcome."

The army kept running. It was Gameknight's plan that they'd go far enough to the west that they could swing around the monster army and sneak into the village. But to do that, they had to move faster than Herobrine expected them to. And for that to happen . . . they had to run!

Suddenly, an Enderman appeared behind the army with two skeletons in his arms. The dark creature dropped his cargo, then disappeared and quickly reappeared with more of the pale, bony monsters. The skeletons instantly began firing at the villagers, their arrows streaking through the air and bouncing off armored bodies, but some pointed shafts found flesh.

Archers quickly formed a line at the rear of the army and returned fire. At the same time, Carver and a group of warriors moved around a hill and surprised them from behind. Carver's shining iron axe carved through the monsters, cleaving multiple skeletons with a single swing. In seconds, the bony monsters were destroyed.

"I don't like this," Gameknight said.

"Why?" Weaver asked.

"These small attacks aren't meant to do any damage. They're just to keep pushing us to the west," Gameknight said.

"But we won every battle," Baker said. "Those monsters didn't have a chance."

"That's just it," Gameknight replied. "They never had a chance. Those skeletons and spiders were completely outnumbered and they knew it, but they attacked anyway."

"The skeletons didn't seem so excited about that battle," Carver said as he returned to the army with his squad of swordsmen and swordswomen. "They kept looking to the south when we attacked. It was as if they were expecting reinforcements, which obviously never came."

"You see, Herobrine is sacrificing these creatures to keep us going west," the User-that-is-not-a-user grumbled. "The questions is: why?"

"I'm not sure we have much choice," Weaver said, pointing to the south.

Gameknight turned to look. The line of monsters still stood just on the horizon, their bodies forming a multicolored row along the savanna. The sun was now high in the sky and beat relentlessly down upon the land, making the hate-filled creatures easy to see.

"Behind us!" someone shouted.

Gameknight turned to the east. Fuzzy black spiders were over a distant hill, flowing over the acacia trees as if they were twigs in a raging river. More spiders appeared to the north; not as many as those to the east, but there was no way the villagers could head for the smaller group without the larger one catching them.

"It seems we have no choice," Baker said, her bright-blue eyes filled with worry. "Herobrine seems insistent we continue to the west."

"I think you're right," Gameknight replied. "If we're gonna be pushed to the west no matter what, let's see if we can get there before their trap is ready. Now, what we need is speed. COME ON EVERYONE!"

The warriors beat their swords on their chests as they began to sprint to the west, the sun now at its zenith. Dashing across the savanna, the army took the two monster armies by surprise and quickly left them far behind. Gameknight led them around hills and in shallow ravines whenever possible, keeping their position hidden from their pursuers. It was a hard run with the hot savanna desert sun beating down upon them, but fortunately, clouds were slowly moving in from the east. They all knew the blazing yellow square overhead would soon be blocked and they'd get at least a small amount of relief from the sweltering temperature. After ten minutes of running, Gameknight slowed to a walk and looked back along their path. No monsters were visible anywhere . . . perfect.

"Since we can't see them, they can't see us," Gameknight said.

More clouds moved in, dropping the temperature even more. Many of the villagers seemed relieved when the cool air finally hit their sweaty bodies, and some smiled for the first time since leaving the birch forest.

Gameknight looked around, thinking this part of the savanna they found themselves in looked strangely familiar. Something about the terrain reminded him of Herder, his friend from the future, as well as Cobbler, the young boy whose village had been taken by the zombie king. It seemed so long ago when that had occurred, yet it also wouldn't happen for another hundred years. . . strange. Then he realized what it was: the savanna village to the south was the one Cobbler had taken them to, only he couldn't remember why. There was a river just on the other side of the next hill, and . . . something else, he couldn't quite recall.

"We need to do what Herobrine doesn't expect," Gameknight said as he focused back to the task in front of him. He glanced at Baker and Carver, who were now running side-by-side. "We're going to start veering to the north, in hopes of attacking that small group of spiders."

The two leaders smiled and nodded their blocky heads.

But just as they started to move northward, a hideous catlike yowl filled the air. Gameknight glanced around, looking to see if it came from behind. The sound was heard again, but this time there was an evil baby-like cry on top of the feline howl.

The noise wasn't coming from behind or from the north or south. It was coming from straight overhead. Directly above them, a massive cluster of ghasts descended from strange-looking clouds. They each had a hateful, evil look to them, their innocent baby-like faces completely erased and replaced with terrifying expressions out of some kind of nightmare.

"OINK, OINK!" Wilbur squealed as the monsters began forming fireballs beneath their tentacles.

"GHASTS!" Weaver yelled as he scooped up the pig and ran.

As Gameknight stared up at the monsters, he saw three massive fireballs heading straight for him. Fear pulsed through every nerve in his body and overwhelmed his mind. As he watched the flaming balls of death descend down upon him, all he could do was stand there and wait for his doom.

CHAPTER 16

WATERFALLS

Time seemed to slow as the fireballs streaked toward Gameknight, the burning spheres growing larger and larger as they approached. Icicles of fear jabbed at him from all sides. His feet seemed frozen and unable to move. He was doomed.

Suddenly, the image of Crafter and Hunter and Stitcher and all his other friends from present-day Minecraft popped into his head. They were looking at him with confidence and hope, as if they knew he could solve any problem he faced. His friends knew he'd never let them down. And at that moment, the fear that permeated every fiber in his body evaporated and was replaced with rage.

"NO!" the User-that-is-not-a-user screamed.

He drew his diamond sword in a single fluid motion and struck the first fireball. It deflected to the side and smashed into a distant acacia tree. Pulling his iron sword from his inventory, he struck the second ball with his left, knocking it away, then hitting the third fireball with his diamond blade. The last burning sphere of death ricocheted off his weapon and shot straight back at one of the ghasts. It blasted the monster in the face, causing it to flash red. A shrill, sorrowful scream escaped the lips of the floating beast just as it tilted over sideways, then disappeared with a pop, its HP consumed.

The villagers cheered, but were quickly silenced when more attacks began from above.

"Everyone, run for the river!" Gameknight shouted.

"River . . . what river?" Carver shouted.

"Just follow me."

Gameknight sprinted across the savanna, heading for the water that would likely save them. Glancing over his shoulder, he saw villagers trying to shoot at the ghasts, but as soon as they stopped to take aim, a barrage of fireballs rained down upon them; none of the lone archers survived the attacks.

"DON'T STOP . . . KEEP RUNNING!" Gameknight screamed.

Another archer turned and fired at a ghast. The giant floating gas bag just rose high into the air, making the shot impossible to make, then fired its own burning projectiles at the villager. Some NPCs were smart and dodged the attack, but most of the warriors that stopped to fight were consumed in flames.

As he ran, Gameknight thought he heard laughter coming from the south. It was the monsters . . . they were laughing at what was happening to the villagers. Endermen were chuckling their high-pitched, screechy laugh, joined by the clattering of skeleton bones and moaning zombies. It added a surreal soundtrack to the horror that was taking place around them as they ran for their lives.

Suddenly, the ground fell away and Gameknight tumbled down a grassy slope, then splashed into a river just as a fireball flew overhead. He'd made it.

Then, right behind him, more villagers were diving into the water and ducking down under the surface, trying to escape the barrage of attacks from the monstrous creatures. Weaver jumped into the water next to him, Wilbur held in the boy's hands. Gameknight saw a fireball sizzling toward them. Reaching out, he pushed Weaver under the water as he dove for safety. The burning sphere smashed into the river and crashed into Gameknight999. The water extinguished the flames from the attack, but he still took projectile damage. Pain erupted through his body as his HP dropped and he flashed red.

Rising to the surface, he grabbed a quick breath of air and glanced around. Many of the villagers were in the water, some looking badly wounded, but at least they were still alive. He glanced to the edge of the river and saw that items lay strewn along the banks, marking where NPCs had perished before reaching safety.

Turning, he looked upstream. There was a faint rumbling that triggered a distant memory. And then it surfaced; he was remembering something from the future, from the present-day Minecraft where he'd come from. He knew now that the river they were standing in led to a set of waterfalls. Behind the falls was a cave; they'd be safe there.

"Come on every . . ." Gameknight started to shout, but was suddenly shoved underwater by Carver's big hand.

Another fireball crashed into the river, narrowly missing Gameknight999, but striking Carver in the shoulder. He grunted underwater as the big NPC flashed red, taking damage.

Swimming to the surface, he found Wilbur bobbing alongside him. He reached out and grabbed the little pig, holding him close.

"EVERYONE, GO UPSTREAM TO THE WATER-FALL!" Gameknight shouted. "Everyone, follow me."

He swam to the bank of the river. Cautiously, the User-that-is-not-a-user climbed out of the water and ran along the bank, staying crouched and making himself as small a target as possible.

Wilbur oinked.

"INCOMING!" someone shouted.

Gameknight leapt into the water and dunked under the surface just as a fireball smashed into the river. He could see the distorted image of a villager standing on the riverbank. He flashed bright for just a second, then disappeared, his HP scorched to nothing almost instantly; another one lost.

More fireballs sliced into the river, cutting through the water until they crashed against the bottom. When the attack seemed to dissipate, the User-that-is-not-a-user swam to the surface. He checked the sky for attacking monsters, then crawled up onto the riverbank and sprinted, the other NPCs following. Ahead he could hear what sounded like thunder. A mist began to fill the air as he moved farther upriver.

"FIREBALLS! LOOK OUT!" Weaver shouted.

Gameknight jumped into the water again and glanced upward. A woodcutter had been in mid-air when the fireball hit him. The doomed soul disappeared just as he was about to drop into what would have been the life-saving water.

"EVERYONE, FOLLOW ME!" he yelled.

"OINK!" Wilbur added.

Gameknight sprinted along the river bank, heading upstream. He could hear the ghasts in the distance; likely they were checking their surroundings to see if any of the villagers had chosen to run away from the river and into the savanna. If any did that, they wouldn't last much longer.

The thunderous roar grew louder as he neared the mouth of the river. Ahead, a waterfall cascaded over the edge of a cliff and into the river, just like he remembered. Gameknight quickly scanned the sky for the terrifying ghasts. He could see them far downstream, searching the savanna. Suddenly, one of them turned and spotted him. It screeched a terrible, high-pitched scream that sounded as if some animal were being hurt.

"They've seen us," Gameknight said. "Everyone, move fast and follow me."

He set Wilbur on the ground just as Weaver approached. In the water, Gameknight saw Carver holding the child, Milky, as the little NPC's mother and father had both been seriously wounded. Reaching out, he helped the stocky villager onto the banks.

"Thanks," Carver replied.

Gameknight nodded his square head, then pulled out a block of dirt and streaked forward. The riverbank walls grew steeper and steeper the further he ran upstream, until they became sheer walls. If the ghasts reached them now, they would be trapped. Eventually, the projectile damage from the fireballs would get them all.

SCREECH! Another of the evil floating monsters cried out, its evil eyes focused directly on the blacksmith.

Gameknight moved along the edge of the river, placing blocks of dirt next to the steep walls. He didn't have many blocks with him, so he had to space them apart as wide as he could. If he ran out of materials, they would be in trouble. The waterfall was maybe a dozen blocks away and the walls here were solid stone. Reaching out, Gameknight999 placed another block of dirt, then jumped to it. Glancing over his shoulder, he saw the villagers following him, terror and grief painted on their square faces.

Placing another block, the User-that-is-not-a-user jumped forward, then put down his last two. He was within two blocks of the waterfall, but had no more cubes of dirt. In a state of near-panic, Gameknight couldn't remember if there was a ledge in the waterfall or if the crashing liquid just fell straight down into the river. The only way to tell was to jump blindly into the water. But if there was nothing to land on, the waterfall would push him downstream, right toward the approaching monsters.

I have no choice, Gameknight thought. *I have to make the jump. If I miss, then it's over.*

Have faith, child, a calming voice said in the back of his head, the lyrical notes of music adding to the soothing words.

"Weaver," Gameknight shouted over his shoulder. "If I make it, have everyone follow me."

"Follow you . . . where?"

"Through the waterfall," Gameknight replied.

"Through the . . . are you insane?"

"Maybe," Gameknight replied.

"Smithy be crazy!" Carver exclaimed. "GO!"

Gameknight set Wilbur on the block at his feet, took a large breath, then jumped.

CHAPTER 17

THE BUTCHER'S BILL

A tidal wave smashed down upon Gameknight as he plunged into the waterfall. He started to fall, and for an instant thought he'd made the wrong decision, but, thankfully, he felt a solid surface under his feet a block down.

There was a ledge—he was safe!

Climbing quickly out of the water, Gameknight stepped through the rest of the waterfall. A wide cave stood before him, its walls hidden in shadows. He placed a torch on the ground near the water, then stood in the light and waved. Instantly, villagers began to leap through the cascading flow.

First to come through was Weaver with Wilbur in his hands. The pig seemed a little upset at the violent shower, but was glad to be away from the ghasts.

"Weaver, move the torch to the back of the cave," Gameknight said. "I'm going back out to check on everyone."

The young boy nodded his head as he lifted the burning light and moved further into the cavern.

Gameknight jumped into the waterfall and landed on a stone block, then jumped again, moving back outside to the path he'd just created. Along the banks he saw villagers struggling to make it toward the waterfall; some of them were limping badly. NPCs had arms around friends and family members and even total strangers, offering help to any that needed it. In the distance, he could see the ghasts glaring at him as they soared through the air, closing in.

"We have to hurry, the ghasts are coming!" Gameknight shouted.

He pulled out his bow and moved downstream. Drawing an arrow back, he aimed well above the distant monster, then released. The pointed shaft leapt off his bowstring and streaked into the air like a missile. It soared in a graceful arc that was almost beautiful as it closed in on its target. The boxy monster closest to the arrow weaved sideways, easily avoiding it.

"What good did that do?" Carver asked.

"If I keep firing, maybe I can slow them down a little and give the others time to get through the waterfall," Gameknight explained. "And by others, I mean you as well! Get through the waterfall now before it's too late."

He drew back another arrow and fired. As it flew through the air, he quickly notched another arrow and let it fly. But, surprisingly, instead of one arrow streaking through the sky, a dozen flew up into the air. Turning, he found Carver standing defiantly next to him, his bow in his strong hands, and a handful of archers joining them along the banks.

"Let's give them another volley," Carver said, his voice booming across the savanna.

More arrows streaked into the air. None of them hit the ghasts, but they forced the monsters to float higher and swerve to the left and right, slowing their approach. Gameknight stepped back and got in line with the other warriors, adding his arrows to theirs, firing as fast as he could.

One of the ghasts, high up in the air, launched a fireball at the defenders.

"Everyone scatter," Carver shouted.

The warriors spread out as the flaming projectile smashed to the ground right where they had been standing.

"Fire back!" Carver yelled.

The archers let loose another barrage, their arrows whistling high into the sky. But in response, more fireballs were fired back. Gameknight glanced over his shoulder to check on the progress of the villagers. Nearly all of them were through the waterfall.

"Some of you go through the waterfall while the rest of us hold off the ghasts," Gameknight said.

The warriors all stood their ground, firing arrows as fast as they could draw and release.

"This is ridiculous!' Gameknight shouted. "We need to get everyone through the waterfall."

A wave of fireballs plummeted toward them. The User-that-is-not-a-user jumped into the river, narrowly avoiding a fireball. As he climbed back to the river bank, he found two piles of items floating just off the ground; not everyone had been as lucky as he.

"Fall back," Gameknight said, then screamed. "FALL BACK!"

The archers slowly walked backward as they continued to fire at the airborne monsters. When they reached Gameknight's hastily built walkway, Carver moved to his side.

"Go through; we'll follow," Carver said.

He gave the User-that-is-not-a-user a shove toward the falls.

"Okay, everyone through the water!" Gameknight yelled, then ran across the blocks of dirt and jumped through the rushing water. When he climbed into the cave, soaking wet, he turned and waited for the others. Carver came through, followed by a woodcutter and a sadler, but then a massive attack of fireballs descended down upon the river. Gameknight and Carver ducked as some of the fireballs flew through the waterfall and smashed into the cave walls. The blast was deafening as flames lit up the opposite side of the waterfall like an inferno of destruction. When the blinding light from the explosive attack finally subsided, Gameknight looked back to the waterfall; no one else was coming through.

"They're gone," Gameknight moaned. "They're all gone."

Carver stood up, then lifted the User-that-is-not-a-user off the ground and carried him to the back of the cavern.

"They were just there," the User-that-is-not-a-user said as tears began to tumble from his eyes, "and now they're gone. They waited to hold off the ghasts so we could get through the waterfall, and now they're gone forever."

Gameknight stood and turned toward the villagers that were huddled at the back of the cave. He could hear cries of grief as mothers and wives realized their loved ones would never return. Villagers in pain moaned as others tended to their wounds and gave them food. It looked as if half the villagers that had followed Gameknight999 into the savanna were gone . . . destroyed by the ghasts in fiery explosions. The stone chamber was consumed with sorrow and grief.

"What have I done?" Gameknight moaned, as guilt over all their despair slammed into him like a sledgehammer.

Wilbur came forward and rubbed himself against Gameknight's leg, then looked up at him. The Oracle then stepped forward, encircled by her light-crafters.

"You did what you had to do, child," she said. "You turned a hopeless situation around and gave everyone a chance for survival. Without you, *all* of us would have been destroyed by the ghasts. If you hadn't known about the waterfall and the fact that this cave was here, then we'd all likely be dead."

"She's right," Baker added, tears streaming down her flat cheeks. "I lost many good friends today, but I know it could have been worse."

"But if I'd just left you alone and stayed away from your village, then your friends would still be here," Gameknight replied in a weak voice.

"True, but for how long?" Baker asked. "Sometimes in life, we don't know in advance what the right thing to do is. Maybe go left, maybe go right, maybe go nowhere . . . it's hard to tell. If I think about what's best for my village and focus on what might go wrong, I become paralyzed and can't make any decisions; I feel lost."

"What does that . . . have to do with any of this?" Gameknight asked.

"Smithy, when you came to our village and asked for our help, I had that same moment of feeling lost," she explained. "I didn't know what to do: Should I follow you on this dangerous course, or should I hide in my trees and hope the storm just blows past us?"

"So how did you choose?" Gameknight asked. "What made you decide to go with us?"

"I did what I always do when I feel lost," Baker said. "I just stopped, closed my eyes, and listened."

"Listened to what?" he asked.

"I listened to Minecraft and I listened to myself," she replied. "And you know what I heard?"

By now, the cave had become completely quiet as all the villagers listened.

"What?" Gameknight pleaded. He desperately needed something to give him hope again. "What did you hear?"

"I heard music," she said, a smile slowly growing on her square face as she remembered the moment. "I heard the music of Minecraft. It was the most soothing and beautiful thing I've ever heard."

Gameknight cast a glance at the Oracle, but she was staring intently at Baker.

"But not only that, I heard myself think through the problem clearly, without worrying about what might happen if I made the wrong decision. I heard my true self, without any insecurities or fears or doubts. And my true self told me it's always an honor to be given the opportunity to help another, even if it's difficult or dangerous. Herobrine must be stopped, and if not now . . . when?"

"Your friends, though, they're gone . . . because of me," Gameknight said.

"No, my friends are gone because of those ghasts and because of Herobrine," Baker growled. "Villagers help villagers. That's the way it's always been, even if it's difficult or dangerous, and that's the way it's gonna be in the future."

She took a step forward, standing next to Carver and stared at Gameknight999, determination etched onto her square face.

"Smithy, you asked yourself, 'What have I done?'" Baker said. "Well, you turned certain death into a chance for life for everyone in this chamber."

Carver nodded in agreement.

"Oink!" Wilbur added.

Baker reached down and petted the pink animal on his head.

"You seem to know the most about this Herobrine character," Baker said. "You're gonna figure out our next move, because we sure aren't gonna sit around in this cave feeling sorry for ourselves. We need to take decisive action. Herobrine and the ghasts probably think we've been almost completely destroyed. Maybe he even thinks you're dead. That means we now have the advantage of surprise."

"I don't know," Gameknight moaned. "I can't be responsible for more deaths."

"You aren't . . ." Baker said. "Here, let me make it easy for you. Everyone who is willing to follow Smithy and continue the fight, step up."

At first, no one moved. Gameknight's head began to droop a little as hopelessness set in. Then Carver moved to Gameknight's side, followed by Baker. The Oracle shuffled across the stone floor, followed by her light-crafters. They stood close around Gameknight999, Treebrin's rough, bark-like skin scratching his leather armor. The User-that-is-not-a-user smiled at those around him and was about to say something when everyone huddling in the darkness came forward, each tear-stained face trying to stand tall and be close to Smithy of the Two-swords.

All of the villagers reached out and tried to touch him, creating a massive collective group-hug as the NPCs began to weep again. But this time, the tears of despair were mixed with tears of hope.

"Our loved ones did not die in vain," one of the villagers said.

"The fight isn't over," another growled.

"We aren't gonna give up," someone demanded.

"Smithy can find a way."

"Herobrine will be stopped!"

More comments echoed off the stone walls of the cave as the villagers put their inner thoughts to voice. And this gave Gameknight999 something he hadn't had for what seemed like an eternity: hope.

If these people believe in our cause this much . . . and believe in me, then maybe we can do this after all, if we do it together, Gameknight thought.

That is the wisest thing you've thought in a long time, child, a scratchy voice said in his mind.

Gameknight smiled.

"We sort of look like a massive mountain of villagers all grouped together like this," Weaver said near the outside of the group. "I feel like we could almost reach up and touch the clouds."

"Yeah!" the others said, their sadness now replaced with hope and determination.

"Mountain . . . clouds," Gameknight said.

"What is it?" Carver asked.

But the User-that-is-not-a-user did not reply. He could feel the puzzle pieces tumbling around in his head. There was a solution here, he just needed to set aside his doubts and fears, and rely on those around him.

And then the first puzzle piece fell into place. It was a mountain, a massive mountain, the tallest in Minecraft. He knew exactly where it was, for he'd been there before. They had to go there and figure out what was happening with these ghasts. After they gathered some information, then they could devise a plan, but first they needed to understand the mystery of the ghasts. And to do that, they had to go to Olympus Mons.

CHAPTER 18
DISAPPOINTMENT

As the sun rose in the east, painting the sky with splashes of orange and crimson, Malacoda slowly floated away from Herobrine's army, and moved toward the distant waterfalls. One of his ghasts was arriving to report on the situation, and he wanted to hear the news far from Herobrine's ears.

A cat-like cry floated out of the sky. He glanced upward and saw ghasts moving overhead, dragging their tentacles through the shimmering clouds as they replenished their HP. The sparkling clouds, with the faintest touch of orange, drifted overhead as glowing embers danced along their misty edges. The mountain at Dragon's Teeth was continually generating new infected clouds, which were spreading out all across the Overworld, corrupting all they touched, and extending Herobrine's power across Minecraft.

I'd much rather be up there in the clouds, the monster thought to himself. But he first had to learn what had happened with the blacksmith.

The commander from the waterfalls approached, the evil-tainted ghast giving off cat-like cries and wails that made him sound nervous as he drew near. Malacoda had ordered the ghast to report at sunrise and tell him what had happened with the foolish NPCs. The white ghast approached cautiously, as if it wanted to flee; this did not suggest the monster had good news to share.

"Sire, you asked for an update at sunrise," the ghast said in a baby-like voice.

"What news do you have about the blacksmith?" Malacoda asked.

"We believe our attacks have destroyed him," the ghast said. "Ghasts moved up close to the waterfalls and bombarded them with our fireballs. Since that attack, we spread out around the falls and watched to make sure none emerged from tunnels and tried to escape. There has been no activity or movement since. I'm sure they are all destroyed."

"Did any try to escape?" Malacoda asked.

"None," the ghast replied tentatively.

The fool! Malacoda thought. *That likely means they have escaped. Herobrine will be furious.*

"This sounds like excellent news," the ghast king lied. "I command you to report this to Herobrine."

The king of the ghasts saw a nervous expression flash across the pristine white face of the monster; he knew this was not a reward, but a punishment.

Moving behind the monster, Malacoda pushed the monster downward, toward the collection of creatures that congregated on the savanna. The ghast floated hesitantly forward, the pressure of Malacoda's tentacles on his back keeping him moving forward.

Gracefully, he floated downward toward a clearing ringed with acacia trees. Zombies moaned and growled in one section near a tall, twisted tree, while skeleton bones clattered in another. A ring of fuzzy black spiders surrounded the group: the outer guards. Farther out in the woods, Endermen zipped about like shadowy streaks of lightning as they teleported through the forest, watching for an NPC attack.

At the center of the clearing, Malacoda saw Herobrine standing next to Erebus, the Enderman king and Shaikulud, the queen of the spiders. Malacoda pushed the ghast commander toward the Maker with one of his strong tentacles. They slowly lowered themselves to the ground.

"Maker," Malacoda said, his voice booming across the landscape. "This ghast has something to report."

Herobrine looked up, an excited look on his square face. The ghasts settled to the ground before the evil virus. With the flick of a tentacle against the back of his subject, Malacoda urged the monster to tell Herobrine what had happened.

"We attacked over and over again, firing hundreds of fireballs at the waterfall," the ghast explained. "I know the flames would have been extinguished, but we would have still done damage to the villagers. None in the cave behind the waterfall could have survived. We saw no one leave. That means they are all destroyed."

"You mean to tell me that none of the villagers tried to escape?" Herobrine asked. "Not a single one?"

The ghast nodded and tried to move back, but Malacoda was right behind him, laughing quietly.

"And you didn't think that was strange?" Herobrine asked.

The ghost said nothing.

"Why didn't you ask for help?" the Maker growled, his eyes glowing bright with anger. "We could have sent some zombies or skeletons in there."

Again, the ghast said nothing.

"You fool," Herobrine snapped. "They escaped somehow."

"But we saw no sign of them emerging from the waterfall. There was only a single narrow entrance, and we kept watch over it day and night. There is still a torch burning inside the cave . . . they must still be there."

"You're an idiot! Do you think the blacksmith is stupid enough to use the same path out that he used to go in? They probably tunneled and emerged out of a hole somewhere far away from you."

The ghast moved back slowly, but Malacoda's eyes grew bright with rage, warning the monster if he retreated any more, he would receive a lethal response.

"That cannot be, Maker," the doomed monster implored meekly. "We hovered about and watched the landscape all through the night. Ghasts threw their fireballs all around to light the terrain. No one was seen escaping."

"You let them get away!" Herobrine screamed, hot rage burning within him like a million suns. His eyes blazed. "How can you be so idiotic?!"

"They must still be there," the ghast pleaded. "They could not have escaped. I put ghasts all around that waterfall and we kept vigilant watch. The NPCs are still hiding in there. They must be."

"You fool," Herobrine growled. "They're gone already. I told you, as soon as the blacksmith was spotted to destroy him. If he tried any of his tricks, you were to notify me. You're as stupid as you are careless."

"But I did everything right," the ghast said, his narrow eyes filled with desperation. "We had them trapped."

Herobrine sighed.

"The feeling of disappointment I have over your failure makes me feel. . . ." He paused as he took a step closer to the ghast. "Makes me feel. . . ." He moved even closer. "Makes me feel . . . furious!"

He drew his sword and in a single, fluid motion struck at the monster, but the ghast was expecting this and quickly floated upward into the sky, away from Herobrine and his shining iron blade. The Maker flashed a glance at Malacoda; the king of the ghasts was ready. He had been forming a massive fireball during the exchange, getting ready for the inevitable outcome. It hovered amidst his tentacles, growing larger and hotter. He sucked the ball of fire into this body, then spat it at the pathetic monster. The flaming sphere struck the creature in the back, making it flash with damage. Before it could turn, Malacoda launched two more fireballs at the doomed ghast, burning away its HP until it disappeared with a *pop*, leaving three balls of XP to fall to the ground.

Herobrine looked up at the king of the ghasts and smiled, nodding his square head as his eyes slowly grew dim. He turned and faced the queen of the spiders.

"Shaikulud, send out your spiders," Herobrine commanded. "I want the blacksmith found!"

"Yessss, Maker," she replied, her eyes glowing an angry purple.

Herobrine turned back to Malacoda.

"Go back to the waterfall and find their trail. Those NPCs must not escape. The blacksmith must be destroyed as an example to the rest of the villagers."

"Yes, Herobrine."

"Take some Endermen with you," the evil shadow-crafter continued. "When you find him . . . and you *better* find him, you will send the Endermen back to notify me. Do you understand?"

"Yes, Maker," the king of the ghasts replied.

"Good, now GO!"

Malacoda nodded his large head, then drifted into the sky as an Enderman teleported beneath him, his dark head looking up at the monster. As he drifted to the west, he watched as three Endermen teleported from place to place, keeping up with him. Malacoda smiled at the way he'd handled the situation. If he'd taken the report to Herobrine himself, he would have likely been the one punished, but by letting the commander of the squad give the report, Malacoda successfully shifted the blame . . . and potentially lethal punishment.

He laughed a high-pitched, feline-like chuckle, then drifted faster to the west to begin hunting their enemy, the blacksmith.

CHAPTER 19

DESERT TEMPLE

During the massive barrage of fireballs from the ghasts, the villagers had moved to the tunnels near the back of the cavern. They were all surprised that Gameknight had already known of the passages; the impenetrable darkness at the rear of the cave made them nearly invisible.

Once the fiery attack was over, and night had settled over the land, the villagers had slipped quietly into the waterfall and floated down the river all throughout the night, staying submerged for as long as possible. As Gameknight had expected, the ghasts had left the waterfall to prowl across the savanna, looking for anyone trying to run away. With the monsters far from the river, and the cloud cover blocking the moon from lighting the terrain, they were able to swim away to safety.

They floated along the river until sunrise. In the morning sun, when they could finally see the land around them, the villagers found themselves in a mesa plateau biome. Broad strokes of color and layered clay adorned the landscape, creating a sur-real view.

"It's time to travel on land now, I think," Gameknight said as he made his way to shore.

"Oink," Wilbur said as he followed.

"Yeah, I'm tired of being cold and wet as well," Gameknight said to the pink little animal.

The User-that-is-not-a-user climbed out of the river and moved quickly up a nearby hill. Turning in a slow circle, he checked their surroundings. The orange-red light of dawn was spreading across the landscape, shading the already-colorful terrain with a crimson hue. Around him, red sand covered the ground as far as he could see. In places, white, gray, and brown clay filled the sides of hills in layers, giving the biome a striped appearance. It was fantastic to behold.

Glancing skyward, Gameknight noticed the sky was free of clouds, which also meant it was free of ghasts . . . for now.

He moved down the hill and helped others out of the river and onto dry land. Carver sent scouts out around them, making sure there were no monsters about.

"You think the NPCs in that huge village in the savanna will be okay?" Weaver asked.

"I don't know," the User-that-is-not-a-user replied. "I'm sure they saw the attack from the ghasts. Hopefully, they escaped before Herobrine extended his evil touch to them."

He glanced at the villagers that stood around him. They were all exhausted from the night's ordeal, but there still remained an expression of determination on all their square faces.

"Maybe putting some scouts up there on the pla-teau might be a good idea," Gameknight said, pointing to the tall, flat-topped structure nearby. He glanced to the sky again, determined to keep watch, then continued. "We're heading to the west from here, and we'll follow the edge of that plateau for a while."

Carver nodded and gave out the commands.

Gameknight glanced up at the sky yet again, searching the distant horizon for clouds.

"Why are you continually looking up at the sky?" Weaver asked.

"The clouds back at the waterfall, did you notice how they looked . . . different?" Gameknight asked.

"Sure, they had crazed ghasts coming out of them," Weaver said. "I'd think the ghasts are a bigger concern than the clouds."

"Ghasts, I understand," Gameknight said. "But clouds should always look the same, and I think there was something, I don't know . . . strange about them."

"I thought I saw sparks coming from one of them," Baker said.

"You mean the sparks were coming from the ghasts?" Weaver asked.

"No, from the clouds," the woman replied. "I thought I saw something sparkling in the clouds, as if they were on fire, which . . . I know, doesn't make any sense."

"Maybe it was just from the ghasts," Carver suggested.

"No, it was from the clouds. I'm sure of it," she replied.

"That's exactly why we need to get to Olympus Mons, to look at the clouds," Gameknight said. "It's the highest mountain in Minecraft, and, from up there, we'll be able to get close to the clouds and really see what's going on."

"Do you know where this mountain is located?" Carver asked.

"Well, I can sorta feel if we're going in the right direction or not," Gameknight said. He moved closer to the two NPCs and spoke in a low voice. "Just between you and me, I think the Oracle is somehow directing me to it. I've asked her, but she won't discuss it. She just says, 'Take the advice of Baker, and listen to yourself and listen to Minecraft.' That's all she'll tell me."

Gameknight sighed a frustrated sigh. Suddenly, Carver slapped him on the back and laughed.

"Then maybe you should just take the Oracle's advice and do it, Smithy," the big NPC said.

Baker glanced at Carver, then gave Gameknight a smile and chuckled. With her laughter filling his ears, she moved to an elderly villager and put her arm around the old man, helping him to walk.

They walked quickly through the mesa, their eyes focused around the multicolored terrain but also up toward the sky. Moving along the flat landscape, the army made good time, passing through the plateau before noon. They next headed into a Bryce biome. Tall, multicolored spires reached high up into the sky, each a different shape and height, but the layers of color were all the same. It was as if this entire biome was made by putting layers of colored clay and sand down across the entire area. Then a sculptor had carved the land, digging out valleys and ravines, leaving behind the plateaus and plains and tall spires in the Bryce. It was fantastic.

Traveling through the twisting, narrow valleys slowed their progress a bit. Baker suggested they go to the top of the canyons and head across the flat plateaus, but Gameknight remembered back to a time when spiders in lands similar to these had trapped him. They'd been traveling across the plateaus when the spiders saw them and gave chase. Without the help of Butch and his warriors, Gameknight and his friends might have been in serious trouble back then . . . although, technically it hadn't happened yet, and wouldn't for a long time. The whole time travel thing was still confusing.

His friends . . . he missed them, he realized. Glancing at Weaver, then Baker and Carver and little Milky, Gameknight understood how important all these people were. If the past was inadvertently altered, it might change the future and hurt his friends. The pressure was almost too much to bear.

Just then, a hand settled itself on his shoulder. Turning, he found Carver walking next to him, a reassuring smile on his square face.

"You're looking kinda serious," the big NPC said. "Everything okay?"

"Yeah, just worrying," Gameknight replied. "When I think, I sometimes focus on all the bad *what if's* that could happen, and it makes me a little scared."

"Then maybe you shouldn't do that," Baker said from behind.

She moved up next to Carver. Gameknight saw their arms brush against each other momentarily. The stocky NPC smiled slightly.

"When I have a problem I'm dealing with," Baker continued, "instead of focusing on the bad part of the problem, I think about what I'm going to learn when I solve the problem. That's how we ended up in the trees instead of walled up in our village."

"So your problems end up teaching you something?" Gameknight asked.

"Yep," Baker said with a smile. "Problems are only an opportunity to grow. What can be better than that?"

"How about not having a massive army of monsters chasing us across Minecraft?" Weaver suggested.

The boy had snuck up behind them and was now next to Gameknight999, Wilbur carried in his arms.

"Oink," the pig added; it made everyone smile.

"I think from here we go northward," Gameknight said. "I know there is a savanna village to the west. We could use their help, if they're willing."

"No problem," Carver said as he pulled his big, shining axe out of his inventory. "I'll convince them to help."

"You can't beat them into submission," Gameknight warned. "They need to help because they think it's important, not because they're afraid of you."

"Okay," Carver replied, rolling his eyes then laughing.

He put away the tool, then glanced at Baker. They both held each other's gaze longer than normal. Then the stocky NPC smiled and ran off to the west in search of aid.

"He can't go alone," Baker insisted. "That doesn't seem like a good idea."

"I agree," Gameknight replied.

He glanced at two warriors and motioned them to follow. They sprinted after Carver, their armor clanking as they ran.

"Don't worry," the User-that-is-not-a-user said. "They'll take care of him."

"Who said anything about being worried?" Baker complained as she blushed.

Gameknight watched the three NPCs disappear behind the curving passages as they headed to the northwest. In his gut, he knew this was the right direction to go, somehow. Glancing at the Oracle, he gave her a questioning glare. She smiled, but said nothing.

They finally came to the end of the mesa and entered into another desert biome. This was a hilly terrain, with huge sand dunes and mountains that sometimes blocked their path. Weaving their way around the obstacles, Gameknight drove the NPC army hard. He wanted to get to Olympus Mons as soon as possible, so he could see what was happening in Minecraft.

Leading the army around a large sandy mound, Gameknight saw a familiar structure slowly coming into view: a desert temple. The pyramid-like structure stood majestically on the sand, with a pair of tall square towers on either side of the main entrance. Orange blocks decorated the sides of the towers, giving the structure an almost Egyptian look.

"Come on, let's see what's inside," Gameknight said.

He sprinted to the entrance of the structure and went in. Columns of sandstone lined the edges of the interior, with four tall pillars at the center of the room. Orange blocks decorated the floor, creating a geometric pattern that made the place seem ancient and mysterious.

Turning to say something to Baker, he was surprised to find he was alone in the temple. The User-that-is-not-a-user went back to the entrance and motioned the others inside.

"Come in and get out of the sun," Gameknight said. Tiny square beads of sweat were forming on his face, and he noticed the others were getting hot, too.

"These places are haunted," Baker protested. "All of us are afraid."

"They just have some simple traps in them," Gameknight explained. "I can show you all how to disarm them, then take the loot in the chests. Come in and I'll show you."

"I could use some loot," Weaver said.

The young NPC set Wilbur on the hot sand and went inside, the pig following close behind. Gameknight gave Baker and the others a questioning glare.

"Even the pig is unafraid," he pointed out.

Baker sighed, then nodded her head and went in.

Gameknight explained what he knew about underground rooms that could be found in temples. He dug a hole through the floor, then carved steps into the walls as he descended to the floor far below.

"You see this pressure plate?" he explained as he worked. "If you step on that, it detonates all the TNT that is buried under the floor. As long as you don't step on the plate, you're alright."

A few of the villagers came into the pit and looked at the chests, taking loaves of bread and iron ingots from the stash.

"You see, they aren't haunted," Gameknight said. "You just need to—"

"SPIDERS!" one of the NPCs yelled.

Gameknight glanced at Baker.

"That's Stonecutter," she said, looking worried. "I had him go to the top of the temple to keep watch."

Suddenly, the villager was at the edge of the pit, staring down at them.

"A bunch of spiders are coming this way. They look like they're combing the land in search of us, taking a zigzag path across the biome," Stonecutter said. "They'll find us eventually."

We can either try to avoid being seen, or stand up and fight until none of those spiders are left alive, Gameknight thought. *If we fight, then I have to come up with a battle plan. But what do we do to give ourselves the advantage out here in the open?*

He hated making these decisions alone. If he made the wrong choice, some of them, or all of them, could get hurt. He felt so lost.

And then the music of Minecraft flowed through the temple like a calming breeze.

"How many are there?" Baker asked.

"Maybe twenty or twenty-five," Stonecutter replied.

"That's not so many," Weaver said optimistically.

"But look around you," Baker replied. "*We* aren't so many either, and many of those around you are already wounded." Baker turned to Gameknight999. "Smithy, what do we do? They'll be here soon."

The lyrical tones spread through the temple, growing louder and more beautiful. It brought a sense of peace to all the villagers, but more importantly, it pushed back on Gameknight's fears and allowed him to think.

Suddenly, a memory of his family's last summer vacation popped into his mind. They'd seen prairie dogs in the southwestern United States, the animals' cute little heads popping up out of holes in the desert, then darting back underground whenever a predator was near.

That's what we need to be . . .

"Prairie dogs. We'll be prairie dogs," Gameknight said, shocked when he realized he'd actually said it aloud.

"What?" Weaver asked.

"Never mind," Gameknight replied. "I have a plan, but instead of everyone just doing it, I want to know your opinions. I want feedback, I want your clever ideas."

And so he explained his idea, and some of the NPCs nodded their heads, while others objected and made other suggestions.

"No, not sand, it must be sandstone!" Baker insisted.

"Of course," Builder replied.

"She's right. We can take the sandstone from inside the temple."

"Okay, so we're agreed?" Gameknight asked.

The NPCs all nodded their heads.

"Weaver, you sure we have enough?" Gameknight asked.

"I think so," the young boy replied.

"Okay, then all we need to decide upon is the bait, and I think we all know who that needs to be," Gameknight added.

"Smithy be crazy, that's for sure," Weaver said.

The villagers laughed.

"Let's get to work," the User-that-is-not-a-user said. "We only have maybe thirty minutes before they're here."

Then the villagers all got to work. As they dug, Gameknight moved to the top of the temple and watched their efforts. Suddenly, the Oracle was at his side.

"You think this is going to work?" he asked.

"I don't know, child," she replied. "You just need to trust your friends and let them do their best, so you can do *your* best."

"I suppose," he replied. "But I'm concerned about Fencer and the other villagers. How are they going to know where we are? I think we'll need them with us before this is all over."

"Then perhaps you should tell them where you are," she said.

"How am I going to do that?" Gameknight asked.

"I'm sure you'll figure it out, child," the old woman said. "Sleep on it and maybe you'll come up with a solution. But right now, me and my light-crafters need to get into our positions."

Gameknight watched as the old woman moved carefully down the side of the sandstone pyramid, leaving him completely alone.

"Oink!" He looked down and found Wilbur at his side.

Reaching down, Gameknight patted the little pink animal on the head.

"I'm glad you're here, Wilbur," the User-that-is-not-a-user said to his friend. "I'm not ashamed to say, I'm really scared. If this doesn't work, then we'll all be in serious trouble."

"Oink, oink," Wilbur said, then nuzzled his head against Gameknight's leg.

He patted the pig on the side, then came up with an idea.

"If we're going to face this mob alone, then let's have a little fun."

"OINK!"

But despite his best efforts, icicles of fear began to stab at him from all sides, as the faint wave of clicking floated in on the wind.

"Oink," Wilbur said, a trickle of fear in his tiny pig voice.

"I know, boy. They're coming." Gameknight drew his two swords and waited as waves of dread crashed down upon both of them.

CHAPTER 20

PRAIRIE DOGS ATTACK

The spiders flowed across the sand dunes like a black tide of angry red eyes and razor-sharp claws. Their clicking became louder and louder as they approached, until the sound was nearly unbearable. Gameknight peeked around a sandstone block and watched cautiously, getting ready.

"Wilbur, go up to the top and make some noise."

The pig turned and ran up a set of sandstone steps to the top of the square towers that stood to the side of the temple entrance.

"OINK, OINK!" the pig said.

Wilbur's cries drew the attention of the spider horde, and they stopped their search on the sandy ground to stare up at the little animal. Gathering every bit of courage, Gameknight casually climbed the stairs and stood at the animal's side.

"Now Wilbur, that's no way to speak to our guests," Gameknight said, his voice loud enough for the monsters to hear. "It's not their fault that their queen, Shaikulud, is a coward and afraid to join her pathetic spiders here. Most cowards hide in dark caves. I'm sure she's doing the same."

The spiders began clicking even louder, then charged forward, fury burning in their red eyes. Gameknight picked up Wilbur and ran down the stairs, then entered the temple from the tower door. He sealed it after stepping through, then dashed down the stairs to the ground floor.

A huge section of floor was now missing, exposing the deep pit that was once hidden under the temple. The User-that-is-not-a-user moved along a one-block wide path, and stood on a lone square of sandstone over the center of the hole. Pulling out a shovel, he quickly broke the sandstone path just as the spiders entered the temple. Their clicking echoed off the ancient walls of the structure, anger filling every set of their burning eyes.

Needles of panic stabbed at him, telling him to run, but the User-that-is-not-a-user held his position. He had to stick to the plan; the others were counting on him. And regardless, there was no place to run to . . . he was quickly becoming surrounded by a swarm of lethal spiders.

With just the single entrance, Gameknight had to wait for all of them to enter; he wanted all of the spiders close to him. The monsters glared from across the open space, every one of them wanting to tear at him with their wicked, curved claws. Wilbur, being held under one arm, oinked angrily at the spiders; it made Gameknight laugh.

"Are you all here?" the User-that-is-not-a-user said. "It took you long enough, but none of you are very bright, are you?"

"You sssspeak bravely when you're out of reach," one of the spiders said.

"Why don't you get a little closer, then?" Game-knight asked. "I'd like to see you come and get me."

With the shovel still in his hand, he broke the sandstone under his feet and fell straight down. It felt like slow motion as he plummeted to the bottom of the pit. He knew if he was off by just the smallest amount, he might not survive. But his fears were washed away when he landed directly in the center of a single block of water, the liquid cushioning his fall. Climbing out, he set Wilbur down, then filled the water in with sand.

"Come on down . . . if you can climb those steep walls, that is," Gameknight said, then laughed.

"Fool," the spiders said. "We can climb thesssse wallssss with easssse."

The spiders flowed over the edge of the pit in a hideous black wave of fangs and claws. Gameknight didn't wait around to watch. Instead, he and Wilbur dashed into a side passage that had been prepared. He placed a pressure plate on the empty squares of sand, then sealed himself inside the tunnel.

Following the short passage, he found a flight of stairs carved into the desert sand. Gameknight and Wilbur climbed steps until they were halfway to the ground floor of the temple, then moved to a half-slab opening and watched as the spiders scurried down the walls. When they neared the ground, the eight-legged monsters paused. The floor was covered with pressure plates, and they knew enough to be cautious. One of the spiders moved down and stepped on one of the stone plates . . . nothing happened.

Gameknight smiled.

Then a few more monsters moved onto the pressure plates . . . still nothing happened.

Gameknight giggled.

Satisfied there was no danger, the rest of the spiders flowed across the floor of the pit and began scratching at the blocks that sealed his escape tunnel.

"Fools," Gameknight whispered, "Apparently those idiotic spiders know nothing about redstone repeaters."

"Oink," Wilbur said in his soft pig-voice.

"Three . . . two . . . one," Gameknight counted, then yelled in a loud voice, "BYE-BYE!"

Balls of fire blossomed into life as the explosives under the floor of the pit detonated, wrapping deadly petals of flame around the hapless spiders. The whole temple shook with the blast, causing sand and dust to fall from the ceiling, momentarily making Gameknight and Wilbur cough.

That was the signal for the others. Inside and all around the temple, NPCs broke the sandstone over their heads and popped out of their little prairie dog holes, storming the temple. Villagers with pickaxes dug holes into the walls of the temple, allowing others to charge in with bows in their hands. The warriors lined the edges of the pit and opened fire on the monsters. Some of the spiders tried to climb the sheer walls to escape the rain of barbed projectiles, but they only made it a few blocks before their HP was consumed. In seconds, the cratered floor of the pit was filled with glowing balls of XP and clumps of white string.

Gameknight and Wilbur followed their tunnel to the surface, then broke the sandstone and emerged on the top floor with the rest of the villagers.

"SMITHY!" the villagers chanted.

Suddenly, a clicking sound filled the air near the tunnel entrance. A lone spider had scurried into the temple to see what had happened. When she saw all of the villagers with bows drawn, the creature quickly turned and fled. Baker rushed after the creature. When she passed through the temple entrance, the NPC held her sword with two hands over her head and threw it at the escaping monster. It tumbled end-over-end as the gleaming blade streaked through the air. It struck the monster in the back, completely destroying the monster's HP. The spider barely had a chance to glance back at her attacker when she disappeared with a pop, leaving behind more glowing balls of XP.

Seeing the creature destroyed, Gameknight ran up the side of the temple and mounted the top of a tower. He gazed out into the desert, looking for any fleeing black dots moving across the pale sand. In seconds, the entire group was outside the temple, staring up at him as if he were crazy.

Suddenly, Baker was at his side.

"What are you doing?" she asked.

"The spiders came from that direction, right?" he asked, pointing to a sandy mountain.

"I think so," she replied.

"If any spiders escaped, they'll probably head back that way," Gameknight said. "Do you see any?"

"I don't know," Baker replied. "Stonecutter, get up here and help us look!"

The stocky NPC climbed the steps and stood next to Baker. The three of them stared out into the hot desert, looking for anything out of place. They scanned the surroundings for minutes, but saw nothing.

Gameknight breathed a sigh of relief.

To the west, the sun was slowly settling on the horizon, casting warm shades of red and orange on the sand.

"It looks like we got them all," Gameknight finally said with a smile.

"Good," Baker replied. "It seems you were just the right bait, and if—"

"Wait," said Stonecutter.

A chill ran down Gameknight's spine. He turned and looked in the direction the NPC was pointing. Far away, on a distant dune, they could see a lone spider scurrying up the sandy face, moving as fast as the creature's eight legs would carry her. The monster stopped for just an instant, then turned back and glared at them. Gameknight thought he could see her burning red eyes, but from this distance, that would be impossible.

"We have to catch that spider," Stonecutter growled.

"She'll tell Herobrine that we're here," Baker said. "We must stop her."

"That's impossible," Gameknight added. "She has a huge head start, and when they're sprinting, spiders are faster than us. We'd never catch her without horses."

"Horses?" Baker asked. "What are those?"

"Ahhhh, nothing, never mind," the User-that-is-not-a-user replied. He forgot that horses wouldn't be added to Minecraft for a while; they were in the early versions of the game. "Besides, it'll be night soon, and the monster will just disappear in the darkness. We'll never catch her."

"So what do we do now?" Weaver asked from the sandy ground.

"We get to Olympus Mons as quickly as we can," Gameknight said. "But you can be sure Herobrine will be right behind us."

"Then I guess we better get moving," Baker replied. "The sooner we get there, the quicker we can end this stupid war."

Gameknight looked down at the Oracle and saw a worried look on her wrinkled square face. So far, throughout this entire adventure, she had never looked scared . . . until now. He climbed off the structure and moved to her side. He glanced around at the faces of the villagers, and saw the same expression—fear. They were all terrified.

"This isn't good, is it?" he asked.

She shook her head. "No, child, I'm afraid it is not."

"Any recommendations?"

"I think you had better contact Fencer sooner, rather than later, and tell him what's going on," the Oracle said.

"But how?"

"Remember . . . sleep on it and I'm sure you'll figure it out," she replied.

"Sleep on it . . . of course," he replied, frustrated that she wouldn't just give him the answer.

"Let's get moving to this mountain," Baker said. "I'm tired of waiting around for things to happen *to* us. It's time we made things happen to *them* instead."

"Yeah!" the villagers shouted.

Gameknight gave the Oracle a grin, then headed to the northwest, toward the distant mountain.

CHAPTER 21

THE ENEMY IS SPOTTED

Malacoda soared high over the forest, his tentacles dangling in the breeze while his hateful eyes searched the landscape for their quarry. To the east, the sun was rising, casting rays of light upon the terrain, causing long shadows to stretch from the base of the trees, giving the ground a striped look. Endermen zipped about across the landscape like little bolts of black lightning, their bodies merging with the shadows and disappearing momentarily, only to reappear again when they teleported into the bright morning light. They, too, searched, but the lanky creatures could only see what was directly in front of them and did not have the view the king of the ghasts had from high in the air. Malacoda could see there were no villagers nearby; this sector was clear.

But the ghast king had been smart, and sent out many of his subjects, with Enderman companions, in different directions to look for the blacksmith. Eventually one of them would stumble upon the villagers.

Just then, Malacoda's acute hearing picked up on the frantic clicking of a spider. The creature sounded weak, and trying to signal any monster that could hear her. Peering at the forest floor, he spotted the dark monster scurrying across the leaf-strewn ground. Slowly, Malacoda lowered himself until he was directly in the monster's path. Extending his long tentacles, the ghast wrapped them around the spider and lifted her off the ground.

"Where are you heading to in such a hurry, little spider?" Malacoda asked.

"The enemy . . . the enemy. He hasssss been found."

Instantly, he dropped the spider as the words felt like an electric shock.

"You found the blacksmith?" Malacoda asked.

"Yessss," the spider replied as she looked up at the floating giant.

"Where?"

"In the dessssert," she replied. "I can sssshow you."

"No," Malacoda snapped. "We must wait."

"We cannot wait," the spider replied. "The queen hassss commanded that . . ."

Malacoda reached out and grasped the monster with his tentacles again and lifted her off the ground. The spider struggled to get free, but his nine writhing arms were like bands of cold steel.

Drawing in a full breath, Malacoda let out a cat-like cry that pierced through the tranquil forest like a rusty knife through flesh. Instantly, Endermen appeared beneath him, their dark heads staring up at him.

"Bring the Maker and the army," Malacoda commanded. "The enemy has been found!"

The Endermen disappeared in a cloud of purple, not waiting for further instruction. They all knew the reward for finding the enemy would be great, and the penalty for *not* finding him was likely death; Herobrine did not tolerate failure.

Suddenly, a huge fog of lavender particles formed between the trees of the forest as the Endermen returned with monsters under each arm. After materializing and depositing their cargo, the dark creatures disappeared again to retrieve more zombies and skeletons. The ghast king admired the efficiency of the Endermen. They had brought hundreds of monsters to the forest in minutes . . . it was remarkable.

Suddenly, a chilling presence materialized on the ground. It was as if every bit of anger and hatred and vile contempt for the living had been focused into one place, directly below him. Instantly, Malacoda knew . . . Herobrine had arrived.

Slowly, he settled to the ground and released the spider.

"Maker," the king of the ghasts said, his voice resounding with arrogance. "This spider has seen the enemy. Rather than allow her to run across the Overworld to report her findings, I stopped her and sent for the Endermen."

"Well done, Malacoda," Herobrine said. He turned to the spider and focused his glowing eyes on the fuzzy creature. "Where did you see Smithy and his rabble?"

"They were in the dessssert, to the north," the spider replied. "We trapped him in a temple, but the villagerssss defeated the rest of the sssspiderssss and esssscaped. I ssstayed far from the battle sssso I could report to the Maker, no matter the outcome."

"You did well," Herobrine said. "Your queen will be proud of you."

The spider beamed with pride.

Herobrine turned to the king of the Endermen.

"Erebus, gather all the spiders and deposit them at that temple," Herobrine said.

"Yes, Maker," the tall monster replied.

The Enderman king gave Malacoda an angry glare, then disappeared, the rest of the Endermen following him, each bathed in a cloud of purple teleportation particles.

"We'll send a small force against them, just to get the battle started," Herobrine explained. "And when they think they have vanquished our army, we'll hit them with the full strength of our forces. Their false sense of victory will make their despair feel that much worse." Herobrine laughed as his eyes glowed bright. "After the battle with our main army, the ghasts will ensnare the blacksmith and present him to me. Malacoda, lead the army to the north," Herobrine said. "We must catch the blacksmith before he gets too far away."

"Yes, Herobrine," the king of the ghasts boomed, his bombastic, overly confident voice filling the forest. "Smithy will not get far. Soon, he'll be cowering before you. With this army of monsters approaching from one direction, and the spiders approaching from another, we'll catch the villagers between us and crush them to dust."

Malacoda laughed a cat-like laugh that filled the air, causing the other ghasts in the area to howl. The king of the ghasts glanced down at Herobrine. The Maker's eyes glowed bright white with excitement, while the ghast's own glowed blood-red. Floating off the ground, he moved to the north, driving the rest of the ghasts as fast as possible.

"Come, my ghasts. We have prey that needs catching," Malacoda thundered.

More cat-like cries came from the floating giants as the whole army moved quickly to the north.

CHAPTER 22
OLYMPUS MONS

The villagers ran through the spruce forest that sat in front of the huge mountain that loomed before them. The tall trees would normally seem impressive, but with Olympus Mons in the distance, everything seemed small and insignificant in comparison.

When Gameknight had been here before, the villagers had told him the mountain's name, Olympus Mons, and he'd thought it was peculiar that it was named after the largest peak on Mars. On the red planet, Olympus Mons measured 16 miles high, with a width of 374 miles. It was the largest mountain ever seen by man. Gameknight learned about it in school, and remembered thinking it was strange that the same name was used in Minecraft. Now he realized that, just like the nickname Smithy of the Two-swords, he himself was responsible for the title, having traveled back in Minecraft's past. How strange it all still was. . . .

The last time he'd been here, there had been a different forest around the mountain's base. That had been when they were trying to stop Herobrine's command blocks, and they'd travelled to the mountain from a different direction. Because it was so gigantic, there were likely many biomes surrounding the monstrous peak.

Ahead, he spotted Baker. Gameknight ran ahead to catch up with her.

"Baker, I never did compliment you on that throw you made at the desert temple," Gameknight said.

"Well, I figured we couldn't let that spider get away."

"You're right. It was exactly the right thing to do." He moved closer to her. "Once, a friend of mine named Digger did the same thing. He saved my life by throwing his pick."

"Really?"

"Yep," Gameknight continued. "I was stuck in a spider web. My feet were caught along with my sword, and a spider was charging straight at me. Digger threw his pick and destroyed the spider before it could reach me with its claws. Your throw reminded me of Digger."

"Smithy, do you think Herobrine is already chasing us?" Baker asked nervously.

"Probably," Gameknight replied. "The spider that escaped has probably already been picked up by some of the ghasts or Endermen or other spiders that prowled the land. I wouldn't be surprised if they were heading straight for us right now."

"But there are only about thirty of us," one of the villagers nearby said. "How are we going to withstand an attack by Herobrine? He probably has hundreds of monsters in his army."

"You're correct, unfortunately. I'm sure they have a massive army," Gameknight replied. "But we have help on the way, so you need not worry."

"Help?" Baker asked.

Gameknight nodded.

"Carver will be here soon with the villagers from the savanna," the User-that-is-not-a-user explained, "and Fencer will be here with forces from our village."

"You were able to contact them?" the Oracle asked.

"Yes, I did as you suggested," Gameknight said. "I contacted him while we slept, using the Land of Dreams to communicate with the other dream walker, Carpenter. They know our location and are running toward us as we speak. I'm sure they'll be here any minute."

This made the villagers relax a bit, but there was uncertainty painted on their square faces still.

"Now, let's get up the side of this mountain and see what we can see," Gameknight999 said.

They moved out of the forest and across the open rocky ground, approaching the foot of the mountain. Suddenly, sorrowful moans began to float up out of the forest.

"Zombies!" someone shouted. "A lot of them."

"Smithy, what do we do?" Builder pleaded.

The clattering of skeleton bones added to the noise of growling zombies, creating a horrible cacophony of sound.

"Skeletons, too!" someone yelled.

"Smithy, what's your plan?" Baker asked.

Plan . . . what plan? He thought. *I hadn't planned that they'd find us so quickly.*

"We can't stay here in the open," Gameknight said. "We need to get to a place that is defensible, and out here in the open is the worst place we can be."

"Then let's get up the mountain," Baker said. "At least we can see them coming."

"Right!" Gameknight exclaimed. "Everyone up the mountain."

The villagers all sprinted forward. It was a huge structure, made of stone and dirt and sand, with small clumps of grass here and there. The sides of the mountain sloped gently upward, creating easy, one-block jumps for the villagers as they ascended.

Gameknight picked up Wilbur and dashed up the mountainside. He found Weaver and handed the pig off, then sprinted up the hill, helping the elderly and wounded as he ran.

The sound of the pursuing monsters grew louder as they crashed through the forest; likely they knew the villagers would be surprised to see them and it would be an easy victory. But Gameknight999 wasn't going to let that happen.

After climbing a quarter of the way up the slope, Gameknight stopped and had the villagers start building defenses. He knew retreating all the way to the top, where there was less land, only made it easier for the monsters to surround them.

Walls began to grow out of the side of the mountain, cobblestone structures with holes for archers and blocks to protect them from skeleton arrows. As the villagers worked, Gameknight moved to the side and watched the forest. Weaver and Wilbur moved to his side.

"Do you see them yet?" Weaver asked.

"No," Gameknight said, "but I know they're there."

"Oink!" Wilbur exclaimed.

Just then, the first of the zombies emerged from the forest and crossed the open ground. It was followed by another, and another, and another, until a massive group of decaying monsters were all heading up the mountainside.

"Weaver, do you have any TNT left over?" Gameknight asked.

"No, I used the last of it at the desert temple," the young boy explained. "All I have are arrows, lots of them, but I don't know if arrows are going to be enough."

Suddenly, a large squad of skeletons stepped out of the forest and began climbing the face of Olympus Mons behind the zombies, their bows singing as they moved.

"Quick, get behind the walls," Gameknight said, pulling Weaver and Wilbur to safety just as arrows began streaking by.

Pulling out his bow, Gameknight found a hole in the wall and began firing, shooting trios of shots at skeleton after skeleton, silencing their bows one by one. But with the storm of monsters climbing the face of Olympus Mons, the villagers just couldn't shoot fast enough. There were far too many for the small group of NPCs to handle. It seemed nearly hopeless.

"Have faith, child," an ancient voice said.

Gameknight glanced to the side and found the Oracle standing at his side.

"Help is on the way," she added.

"Really?" Gameknight replied. "I don't see any."

"Be patient," she said.

"How about having your light-crafters help out?" Gameknight asked.

"Look, they already are."

Suddenly, a cheer went up from the villagers. Gameknight turned and saw long blades of grass growing from the green patches that dotted the side of the mountain. The grass snaked outward and became entangled in the legs of any passing monster, stopping their progress and making them easy targets for the archers. Cacti then grew quickly atop the blocks of sand, their prickly spines poking into nearby zombies, causing them to flash red with damage. The zombies and skeletons now had to navigate narrow courses around these obstacles, staying on stone to avoid the light-crafters' traps.

The sight of the light-crafters' efforts invigorated the defenders. They fired their bows even faster, destroying the wounded and ensnared. Angry growls, cries of pain, and the clattering of bones filled the air as the villagers' arrows rained down upon the attacking horde. Slowly, the number of monsters began to fall as they ascended the mountain.

"We're doing it!" Weaver cried. "We're driving them back!"

The villagers cheered, then quieted as a clicking sound began to rise from their left. A huge group of spiders burst out from beneath the leafy canopy and charged up the hill, the sloped mountainside an insignificant hurdle to the fuzzy monsters.

"Oh no," someone said. "Spiders."

The dark creatures scurried up the slope and headed straight for the villagers. Some became caught in the grass or were wounded by the cactus, but the onslaught did not stop. Those that became stuck were just trampled over by their own comrades.

How are we going to defend against zombies and skeletons AND spiders? Gameknight thought.

Then, just when it felt like things couldn't get any bleaker, a loud roar came out of the forest. It was not the sound of a monster, or of some kind of terrifying beast, but a roar that instead lifted all the villagers' hearts.

Carver burst out of the woods, an army of villagers on his heels. With his shining axe, he fell upon the spiders, tearing into their HP with swing after swing. He ran through the assembly of monsters, then turned and faced the leading ranks. The spiders, shocked and surprised, didn't know what to do. But before they could make a decision, Carver smashed back into them while the rest of the army from the savanna village crashed into them from behind.

The fighting was fierce as the villagers fought hand-to-claw with the fuzzy monsters, but none of the NPCs yielded. They drove their attack forward, moving around their flanks and surrounding the monsters. With Carver urging them to fight harder, the villagers chiseled away at their numbers until the last of the spiders were destroyed.

A cheer rang out around Gameknight999, Baker's voice the loudest. Maybe there was hope for them after all.

Carver led the army up to Gameknight's position on the side of Olympus Mons, then added his group's bows to the attack. He had arrived just in time, as another group of zombies and skeletons emerged from the forest and charged up the hill. This group was five times larger than the previous group, and silenced the cheers from the villagers.

"That doesn't look good," Weaver said.

"Oink, oink," Wilbur confirmed.

The monsters advanced up the slope, pushing those stuck in the grass aside as they charged forward.

"Open fire!" Gameknight yelled.

Bowstrings sang as the villagers fired as quickly as they could. The zombies ignored the hail of pointed shafts and shuffled up the hill. Their numbers fell, but there were so many of them, it didn't really matter.

"Half of you, draw swords," Gameknight said. He turned to Weaver. "You stay here with your bow!"

He didn't wait for an answer. Instead, the User-that-is-not-a-user drew his two swords and jumped over the wall they'd made, screaming like a madman.

"Look at that!" Weaver shouted. "Smithy be crazy!"

Gameknight999 slashed at the lead zombie in front of him, tearing away its HP in seconds. Spinning to the left, he attacked the next monster, slicing at its decaying legs as he kicked out and knocked even more monsters over.

Something sharp tore into his shoulder, causing pain to explode from the wound. He felt himself flash red as his HP decreased, but when he turned, he found a dozen villagers around him, their swords flashing through the air like iron lightning.

The monsters hesitated for a moment as more villagers climbed over the walls and attacked. A line of fifty villagers stood before the beasts, their swords gleaning in the afternoon light, while archers poured arrows down upon the attacking monsters. Carver's great axe cleaved massive holes in the monsters' ranks, while Baker's sword did a delicate dance of death. She was all grace and finesse, darting here and there like an elegant but deadly ballerina, while Carver was pure brute force. The two NPCs were a fearsome combination, each attack merging with the other like a complicated choreographed dance; they were nearly unstoppable.

Even though the villagers were grossly outnumbered, they did not yield. They fought as if everything depended on their success; but, even still, there were just too many of the monsters, and the bulk of the army came closer and closer, pushing the defenders back against their own wall.

The light-crafters jumped over the wall and added their fists to the battle. Treebrin towered over everyone as his rough, bark-like skin deflected the zombie claws with ease. His dark fists smashed into monster after monster as if he were wielding some kind of mythological warhammer. At his side, Cactusbrin jabbed his spiked fists into the monsters, making them flash red with damage and leaving painful thorns in the monster flesh. Grassbrin moved like greased lightning around the monsters as if he were untouchable. He struck at the creatures with hands that shot out like deadly green snakes. Monsters roared in frustration, turning to see who had struck them, only to be attacked from behind by the other light-crafters. The trio was a deadly combination, but even with their strength, the monsters were still too numerous.

Suddenly, what seemed like a dark cloud flew through the air and landed on the monsters. They screamed out in pain and surprise. Another cloud sailed through the sky and landed on the monsters, making some of the beasts disappear. One of the zombies fell forward, and Gameknight saw it was stuck with multiple arrows.

Arrows? Gameknight thought, and then it dawned on him.

"Fencer is here!" Gameknight shouted.

And at that moment, Fencer charged out of the forest to their right. Their army was a hundred strong, if not more. Every one of them was fully armored and bristling with weapons. They smashed into the monsters' flank, wreaking terrible havoc. The creatures saw the incoming army and tried to turn and flee, but more grass and cactus sprouted up out of the ground, making it difficult, if not impossible, for any of them to retreat.

"Advance!" Gameknight shouted, recognizing they held the advantage.

"Smithy be crazy!" Carver yelled, drawing laughter from the villagers.

"SMITHY BE CRAZY!" the NPCs replied as they charged forward behind their blacksmith.

They pushed the monsters together into a small group, swords tearing through HP as zombies and skeletons disappeared, littering the ground with glowing balls of XP. But just when it seemed as if victory was within their grasp, yet *another* group of monsters shuffled out of the trees and began to ascend the mountain.

"More monsters!" Carver shouted.

"It's too many," Gameknight replied. "We'll lose lots of villagers if we stand face-to-face with them."

"You have a better idea?" Baker asked.

"It depends on whether Fencer brought any TNT with him," Gameknight said.

"I did better than that," Fencer replied. "He's back up there with the Oracle. You should go ask her about him."

Gameknight gave him a confused glance, then turned and surveyed the battlefield. The new monsters were getting closer, while the existing ones continued to fight, the presence of reinforcements giving them strength and courage.

"Everyone, behind the walls," Gameknight said in a loud, commanding voice. "I think we have a surprise for our angry friends."

The villagers cheered, but Gameknight contained his excitement. He knew that if Fencer's plan, whatever it was, didn't work, they'd have to fight the monsters hand-to-hand, and a lot of villagers would not survive that battle.

He shuddered as he ran up the mountainside, the growls and moans of the monsters filling him with dread.

CHAPTER 23

THE FUTURE REPEATS IN THE PAST

Gameknight sprinted up the hill and found the Oracle.

"We need TNT, and lots of it," he said to the old woman. "Fencer said you had something that would help."

"I do," she replied with a smile. "Meet my newest light-crafter, TNTbrin."

A large (actually, there was no other way to describe him but fat) light-crafter stepped forward. He wore a red tunic with bright-white stripes running diagonally across his chest. He was wider than two villagers put together, as if he were about to burst, but also taller than anyone Gameknight had ever seen in Minecraft, including Treebrin. His size would have been terrifying, except there was a huge smile plastered on his square face.

"You need TNT, boy-o," TNTbrin said with a chuckle.

"Ahh . . . yeah," Gameknight replied.

"Well, TNTbrin is here to deliver."

The rotund light-crafter knelt on the ground, then closed his eyes and started to hum. Many of the villagers stopped shooting their bows to watch.

"Keep firing," Gameknight called out to them. "We have to keep the monsters back."

When he turned back to face the strange newcomer, he saw TNTbrin's hands were glowing bright white. Quickly, the light-crafter thrust them into the ground. Instantly, the glow began to spread outward, like water flowing from a leaky bucket. When the white light had spread at least twenty blocks in all directions, TNTbrin grunted once, and the glow became so bright that it obscured the ground. But when the glow receded and he pulled his hands out of the mountainside, Gameknight realized there were now blocks and blocks of TNT right under his feet.

"There you go, buddy-boy," TNTbrin said with a huge grin.

"Quickly, everyone not shooting a bow, dig up the TNT!" Gameknight exclaimed, almost in shock at their turn of fortune.

The villagers put away their swords and pulled out pickaxes. They smashed the blocks of TNT, causing them to shrink and float off the ground. Moving quickly across the mountainside, Gameknight collected as much as he could, then moved to Carver's side.

"We need to hold the monsters here," the User-that-is-not-a-user said. "I need time to get ready. As soon as everything is prepared, you'll need to get out of there, fast."

"No problem," the big NPC said.

Gameknight looked at Carver with a worried expression on his face.

"This is dangerous. I'll need to take most of the warriors with me," the User-that-is-not-a-user added. "You and the others with you will be on your own. But if we can pull this off, then we'll save a lot of lives."

Carver glanced at Baker. She was firing her bow with lethal precision down at the approaching mob.

"Take her with you," Carver said, a look of determination in his eyes.

"Okay."

"Then let's do this!"

Carver picked out twenty-five of the best soldiers and had them stand behind the wall with bows in their hands. Gameknight took the rest higher up on the hill. They had climbed nearly thirty blocks above Carver when he had them stop and build new defenses.

"We need archer towers, with holes in the walls to shoot through," Gameknight explained. "Here we'll make our stand with bows in our hands, and cover Carver's retreat when it's time. Everyone understand?"

They nodded their heads.

"Then start building!" Gameknight shouted. "Baker, Weaver: come with me."

The two NPCs stood at his side. Quickly, he distributed the TNT amongst them, then handed out some redstone torches and explained the plan.

"Do you both have some stone?" he asked.

They nodded their square heads.

"Okay, then spread out and build what I'm building," Gameknight said.

With a stack in his hand, he started building a line of stone straight out in the air in front of him. He didn't go up, or down, he just built out.

Glancing at the others to make sure they were doing the same thing, he kept building until he was directly over Carver's position.

Down below, he could see the monsters were almost on top of the twenty-five defenders. Shouts of pain came from the villagers as skeleton arrows found their targets. A villager disappeared, then another, as their HP was exhausted.

We must hurry, he thought. *They won't last much longer.*

"Carver, get out of there . . . NOW!"

Without looking up, Carver and the surviving warriors turned and ran up the hill. At the same time, the zombies and skeletons swarmed over the walls, completely taking over their position. Arrows streaked at the retreating villagers, but Gameknight's own archers were beginning to fire back, forcing the skeletons to keep their bony heads down.

Reaching into his inventory, the User-that-is-not-a-user pulled out a redstone torch and placed it at the end of his stone path. He then pulled out a block of TNT and held it over the torch, and signaled to Weaver and Baker. The two placed their own redstone torches, as well as blocks of TNT, against the sides of their stone paths. Instantly, their cubes of TNT began flashing and fell downward. As their blocks fell, they quickly added more, so that there were multiple flashing explosives falling at once.

Huge balls of fire erupted on the monsters' left and right flanks, forcing them into the center, where Gameknight was waiting. He placed his explosive cube against the cobblestone path. The redstone torch instantly started the TNT to blink, then fell down amidst the monsters. More explosions filled the air as great fists of flame blasted into the monsters, making some flash red with damage, while others just disappeared completely.

The monsters tried to charge up the hill to get away from the blast. But Gameknight was expecting this and backed up along the stone path, planting a new redstone torch and dropping more TNT onto the monsters. Baker and Weaver followed suit. Each flashing cube burst into life in a terrible explosion, tearing HP from zombie bodies and blasting skeletons apart. The monsters tried to scramble out of the way, but they were clustered so tightly together from Baker's and Weaver's initial assault that they only collided into each other, going nowhere.

Adding more and more of the red-and-white-striped cubes to the attack, the three companions pounded the monsters with more blasts of flame, and their enemy's numbers became significantly reduced. As the smoke from the TNT began to clear, a massive crater in the side of Olympus Mons became visible, with the surviving monsters trying desperately to climb out of it to escape.

Glancing over his shoulder, Gameknight saw Carver.

"Carver . . . ATTACK!"

The big NPC smiled, then shouted so loudly that it made the white clouds overhead shudder in fear.

"Villagers, ATTACK!"

The NPCs put away their bows and drew their swords. Like an unstoppable flood, the villagers charged down the slopes of Olympus Mons and smashed into the surviving monsters. Gameknight watched from his perch as Carver swung his mighty weapon through the violent horde. He smashed into skeletons, shouldering some aside and kicking others to the ground. The iron axe was like a devastating force of nature, wreaking havoc amongst the monsters.

But then Baker was at his side. Gameknight hadn't seen her climb down from their position, but she quickly descended to the battle and began her own delicate dance of destruction. Her sword was like a silvery blur as she slashed at the monsters that tried to sneak up behind Carver.

The villagers pushed the monsters back into the crater that now adorned the mountainside, slowly destroying one after another until the last monster finally disappeared. All that was left behind were hundreds of glowing balls of XP, skeleton bones, chunks of zombie flesh, and clumps of spider silk.

Gameknight breathed a sigh of relief as he descended down to his friends.

"SMITHY! SMITHY! SMITHY!" they yelled as he moved through the crater.

Gameknight found the Oracle standing next to Fencer.

"That was a great victory," Fencer said.

"I'm just glad you came along when you did," Gameknight said. "If you and Carver had been delayed even a minute more, it could have been a very different outcome."

"We came here for a reason, child," the Oracle said, pointing to the peak. "Perhaps you should get to it before it gets too late."

Gameknight cast a quick glance to the west. The sun was about to reach the horizon, and it would be dark soon.

"Right," he said. "Weaver, you and Wilbur come with me. Let's see what it looks like from the top of the mountain."

"Oink," the pig said.

Gameknight picked up his little pink friend and ran up the slopes with Weaver at his side. They moved in lock step up the mountain, jumping exactly at the same time. In thirty seconds, they passed through the cloud layer. It grew colder as they rose higher on the peak, and snow began to cover the ground. The crunch of their feet through the pristine frozen white coating was the only sound they heard; it felt as if they were the only people in Minecraft.

Finally, they reached the top of the mountain, which Gameknight guessed had to be at Minecraft's maximum build height. As he stood at the peak, he looked to the west, toward the setting sun. Pristine white clouds stretched out across the landscape. Ghasts could be seen playing amongst the clouds. None of the monsters had tried to attack them during the battle, which made Gameknight think whatever Herobrine had done to the ghasts, he'd hadn't done it to them all . . . yet.

To the east were more clouds, but instead of them all being a pristine white color, some smaller clouds sparkled and glowed a subtle orange as they moved across the sky towards him. Strangely, Gameknight realized that when the orange-y clouds touched a regular one, it instantly infected it with the same soft, orange hue. And when that happened, the ghasts within those clouds changed from innocent, child-like creatures, to something that looked angry and evil.

"Those orange clouds, they're infecting the others," Gameknight said.

"Yeah," Weaver replied. "It must be something Herobrine's doing."

As he looked to the east, he saw orange clouds all across the horizon, approaching fast. Everywhere in that direction, the entire sky was infected with Herobrine's vile glowing clouds.

"Look what he's doing," Gameknight said, his voice cracking with fear. "He's covering the entire land with his infected clouds. Eventually, he'll control all of the skies, and every ghast will be his to command. Then they'll blanket the land with fire and destruction."

"We have to stop him," Weaver said. "But how?"

"I don't know," Gameknight replied.

Then he noticed one orange cloud that was drawing particularly close. It glowed softly, as if there were fire within its misty blocks, but there was also an insipid yellow color to the glow as well. It reminded him of when Herobrine had tried to transform the Overworld into End stone. That transformation wave had the same pale yellow color to it; Herobrine's viral crafting abilities were likely powering these orange clouds using the same method.

If we destroy Herobrine, maybe the orange clouds will stop this infestation, Gameknight thought.

But as he considered how they could possibly stop him, he spotted movement down in the forest. An army of monsters at least ten times larger than the one they'd just fought was approaching Olympus Mons. It must be Herobrine's real army, he realized, and the one they'd just defeated was nothing more than a scout for the real force. There were hundreds of zombies, skeletons, spiders, and Endermen, and hovering over them was an army of ghasts, their angry, cat-like cries just barely audible on the wind.

"Oh no," Gameknight said as he pointed to the army.

Weaver gasped, and Wilbur gave out a scared oink.

"How do we defeat that?" Weaver asked, his voice shaking with fear.

"I don't know, Weaver," Gameknight replied softly. "I just don't know."

CHAPTER 24

HOWLING OF THE WOLVES

The three companions ran down the hill in complete silence. Both Gameknight and Weaver contemplated the horror of what they'd just seen as they jumped down block after block, descending to their friends below. As they moved down the mountain, shouts of celebration could be heard; the villagers were still enjoying their recent victory.

"I feel bad having to kill their party down there," Gameknight said. "Listen to them."

They could hear singing and cheering and a general celebration for life, and now Gameknight999 knew he had to destroy that moment with news that would crush all their spirits.

"We have to tell them," Weaver said. "What other choice do we have?"

"Oink," Wilbur agreed.

"If we don't, then Herobrine and all those ghasts will get here and it'll all be over," the young NPC added.

Gameknight nodded as he ran down the last few blocks and joined the rest of the army.

"Smithy!" someone shouted.

"SMITHY!" the rest of them cheered.

Hands slapped him on the back and mothers hugged him as he walked through the group. Near the edge of the crater, he saw the Oracle. By the look on her face, Gameknight could tell she knew what was coming. Around her, all of the light-crafters had the same expression on their faces: fear.

"I need everyone's attention," Gameknight said.

The cheering and singing continued. Pulling a block of stone out of his inventory, he jumped in the air and placed it beneath his feet. He then did it again so that he stood towering above everyone. Drawing his diamond sword, he banged it on the stone, causing a spider web of cracks to form on one face.

"LISTEN TO ME!" he shouted.

The celebration instantly stopped as all eyes swiveled to him.

"I'm sorry to put a damper on the festivities, but you need to know what I saw from the top of the mountain," Gameknight said.

Someone placed torches on the ground as the sun sank beneath the horizon, allowing the sparkling stars to emerge on the blanket of darkness that stretched overhead.

"The force we defeated was not Herobrine's real army. It was only their advance group," the User-that-is-not-a-user explained. "His main force is heading right toward us this very instant. It's easily ten times larger than the army we just defeated. Even with all the TNT in all of Minecraft, we couldn't defeat that army here on this mountain."

"We can run away!" someone shouted.

"Yeah, let's retreat," said another.

"They also have ghasts, hundreds of them," Gameknight added. "They'll track us from the sky and follow us until we are cornered. But that's not even the worst part."

"You mean there's *more* good news?" Fencer said, scowling sarcastically.

Gameknight nodded, a solemn expression on his face.

"I've seen what Herobrine's real plan is for Minecraft. He's infecting all the clouds across the Overworld. Every infected cloud is producing evil, infected ghasts. Soon, he'll be able to cover all of Minecraft with ghasts. We can never battle that."

"It's hopeless," someone moaned.

"They'll destroy everything . . ."

"We should just stop trying . . ."

Suddenly, the sound of a stick tapping on the ground brought all eyes toward the Oracle.

"Never give up!" she snapped. "Never surrender! If there is life, then there is hope. I'm sure there is a solution to this problem. We just need to find it."

All eyes turned back to Gameknight999. He could feel the expectation in every pair: Smithy would save them, wouldn't he? He felt their desperate hope, crushing him under the weight of the impossible responsibility he'd taken on.

He jumped off the blocks of stone and sat down, cradling his square head in his hands.

"Child, tell them how to stop all this madness," the Oracle said.

Gameknight looked up to find her by his side, her light-crafters standing near.

"You know what needs to be done, child. You just need to figure out how to do it."

"Game . . . ahh, Smithy, I mean. You know how to stop Herobrine?" Fencer asked. "Tell us . . . tell us what to do."

"Yes, tell us," another villager pleaded.

"Tell us . . ."

"Tell us . . ."

"Tell us . . ."

Gameknight stood and raise his hands, quelling the flood of questions.

Baker put a reassuring hand on his shoulder and spoke softly, her voice calming his fears for just a moment.

"Tell us what you think will help," Baker said. "All of us will do anything you think is necessary to stop this disaster."

He looked up at her and shivered in fear. "Well . . . I think if we destroy Herobrine, then the clouds will stop being infected." Slowly, he lowered his eyes to the ground. "I think that's the only way."

There was the briefest moment of silence, like the chilling quiet before a massive storm, and then the villagers erupted in questions, shouts of fear, declarations of hopelessness, and cries of despair. All around him had a look of confusion and chaos in their eyes, all except Baker and Carver. The two leaders looked at each other, then back to Gameknight999.

"Let's take this puzzle apart, Smithy, piece by piece," Baker said.

Carver nodded.

"I think it's the ghasts," he said, his voice barely audible over the shouts of confusion and fear. "How can we destroy Herobrine when he has all those ghasts?"

"All those flying monsters need to do is raise up into the air to escape our attacks," Baker added, raising her voice so she could be heard. "So maybe we need to keep them close to the ground."

Gameknight looked around him. Everyone looked terrified, except for Baker, and Carver, and of course the Oracle. She wore a knowing smile, as if she was carrying some kind of secret inside her that was burning to get out.

"The other problem is shooting the ghasts," Carver added, his calm voice slowly filling Gameknight with confidence.

"Yeah, it always takes a couple of shots to destroy one," another voice added.

Turning, Gameknight found Fencer and Weaver had joined the discussion, and he noticed that the fear and uncertainty in their eyes was slowly being replaced with determination.

"And they move around so it's hard to hit them a second time," Weaver added. "We need to get them with one shot. . . . But how?"

"I don't know the answer to all of these questions, but I know there is an answer here," Baker said. "We just need to figure it out, together."

Just then, the puzzle pieces began to tumble around in Gameknight's head. He could feel the solution was in there, but with all the possibilities, he couldn't quite see it yet. For some reason, an image of Herder—"the Wolfman," as the warriors of his time called him—surfaced at the top of the confusing haze in his mind.

Gameknight glanced at the Oracle as if she somehow had the answer. Slowly, she raised her wooden cane into the air, then brought it down onto the stone block at her feet. It hit the mountainside with such force that Olympus Mons shook. A bolt of lightning blasted the ground next to her, its bright light and accompanying clap of thunder silencing everyone.

When the bright light faded, a new light-crafter stood on either side of her. One was tall and muscular, with long, sinewy legs that looked as if they could run forever. Long white hair flowed down his back and covered his arms. He had a look of strength and pride, but his tiny black eyes bespoke of danger. This was a creature you did not want as your enemy. The other had a green scaly texture to her arms, with long clumpy green hair falling around her shoulders.

The Oracle looked at her new friends and smiled, then turned toward Gameknight999.

"Allow me to introduce you to my newest light-crafters, Wolfbrin and Leafbrin," the old woman said. "I think Wolfbrin will be able to aid you in your quest, but it'll take some time before his *friends* are ready to help. Leafbrin will prove just as useful, but in other ways."

The wolves, of course, Gameknight thought. *And then we'll use dispensers and pressure plates and. . . .* The ideas flew through him like an unstoppable storm.

Gameknight smiled as the puzzle pieces began to fall into place.

"With all of your help, I think we can come up with a battle strategy that will give us the advantage and destroy Herobrine once and for all," Gameknight said, his voice ringing with confidence.

All of the villagers were gathering around him now, and the fear that had been there only a moment ago was slowly being driven away by the confidence in their leader's voice.

"We're going to play a little game of follow-the-leader with Herobrine and his mob," Gameknight said. "But we need to act fast. We can only do this if we work together."

He moved amongst the villagers, reaching out to touch a shoulder here and an arm there.

"I'm going to be asking all of you to do something that will seem terrifying and fill your soul with fear, but I need you to trust me," Gameknight said. "The only way we can defeat Herobrine is to take him someplace where his ghasts can be neutralized, and he won't have the advantage. We need to take the monsters to an unexpected place where we'll have some surprises waiting for them. But I need all of you to put your fears and doubts aside, and trust me, even if what you see makes you want to panic and run away. You must trust me. Can anyone *not* do this?"

He glanced around at the sea of faces before him. There was trepidation in their expressions; they had heard the seriousness in the blacksmith's words, and were rightfully afraid that he was asking something of them that they couldn't give.

I can't do this without them, Gameknight thought. *What if they won't follow me? What do I do, what do I . . .?*

Suddenly, a strong, proud howl filled the air. Gameknight turned to see that a wolf had appeared next to Wolfbrin; the animal was howling at the top of its lungs, its snout pointed up to the sky. The light-crafter looked down at the animal, then smiled at Gameknight999. Bending his head back, the new light-crafter howled as well, singing to the stars overhead.

Wilbur then began to oink, adding his own little piggy howl to the concert. Weaver joined them, leaning his head back and letting his voice ring, howling as loud as he could. More voices joined the wolf's; mothers, sons, daughters, fathers . . . all of them were howling as loud as they could, the air filled with their strength and pride. The wolf pack of villagers was ready for battle.

Finally, they all stopped and shifted their attention back to Gameknight999, confident expressions on every square face.

"Where is this historic battle to take place?" Baker asked. "It seems we need to prepare."

"Yeah," Carver added. "Where are we going set up our little surprises? I have a few of my own I'd like to add to the mix."

"Where are we going?" asked another, then another, and another.

Gameknight raised his hands for silence, then spoke in a low, serious voice.

"We're going to the Nether."

CHAPTER 25

PREY IS CORNERED

"Why have we been waiting so long!" Herobrine exclaimed. "Where are my generals? Where is Erebus? EREBUS!"

The evil virus paced back and forth impatiently. He wanted to hit something, to destroy something, but there were no monsters nearby, just tall spruce trees. And where was the fun in punching a tree? It would not suffer from his wrath.

He'd arrived to the huge mountain only to find his advanced force had been destroyed by the blacksmith and his NPCs. Herobrine had sent his monster kings out on scouting missions, to learn what happened to the villagers and where they were hiding, but that had been long ago. Now, the Maker was getting impatient.

Suddenly, Erebus materialized in front of Herobrine, the Enderman king's eyes glowing bright red.

"We have them trapped," the dark crimson monster reported.

"What?" Herobrine replied.

"The blacksmith and his rabble destroyed the small army you sent out to greet him," Erebus continued. "And now they've tunneled into the mountain and are hiding inside like a bunch of scared silverfish."

"Have the ghasts begun firing on the mountaintop yet?" Herobrine asked.

"Not yet," the king of the Endermen said. "I told Malacoda to wait for you to arrive and direct the battle."

"Good. That bloated ghast king would probably mess it up."

Erebus smiled, his eyes glowing red with glee as Herobrine chastised the bombastic Malacoda.

"Bring the army to the foot of the mountain," Herobrine said. "But I want the spiders to stay off to the side. Then, when the attack begins, they'll charge in and attack their flank. I want the villagers destroyed as quickly as possible, but Smithy is to be left alive for me. Do you understand?"

Erebus nodded his dark head.

"Good . . . now go."

The king of the Endermen disappeared in a cloud of purple mist, leaving Herobrine alone. Closing his eyes, the virus teleported to the top of a tall spruce tree and looked out at the gigantic mountain before him. It stretched all the way up to Minecraft's maximum build height, a collection of rock and sand and dirt that seemed almost impossibly big. Cacti and long strands of grass decorated a small area of the mountainside where the battle had taken place. A huge crater precisely marked the location; that was where his forces had been defeated.

Herobrine's eyes grew bright with anger. He didn't really care those monsters had been destroyed, nor did he care if the villagers felt momentarily victorious. Soon, the full weight of his army would fall upon them and there was no way they could survive. He was just impatient; he wanted to destroy that blacksmith immediately!

A cat-like cry floated down from overhead. Looking up, he saw his sparkling, infected clouds drifting above him. They had now covered much of the Overworld, from the Dragon's Teeth to where he was standing now, and were beginning to spread even faster and further away. Soon, his glowing orange clouds would be like a suffocating blanket across all of Minecraft.

Someone's watching me, Herobrine thought.

Turning quickly, he drew his iron sword with a fluid, deadly grace. Staring into the trees, he scanned the surroundings, his glowing eyes acting like a pair of angry searchlights, shining harsh white light wherever he looked. But there was no one nearby.

He turned and looked back to the mountain, then had the feeling again that he was being watched. Somehow, now he could tell it was that old hag, the Oracle. She was spying on him. Gathering his viral powers, he teleported to a different tree that stood near the edge of the mountain. He listened for footsteps in the forest, but heard none; the spies must have left.

With a malicious laugh, he teleported to the ground, then walked to the edge of the forest. It loomed high in front of him, the peak pushing through his orange clouds and . . .

There it is again! Herobrine thought. *She's watching me, and they're right behind me.*

He spun around, only to find a large spruce sticking up out of the ground, and no villagers or light-crafters in sight. Moving to the tree, he looked at it up close. The feeling of being watched was coming from the leaves on the tree. Somehow, she was spying on him through the trees . . . how was that possible?

"You want to watch me, Oracle?" Herobrine growled. "Fine, then watch this."

Reaching out with a dark hand, he touched the side of the tree, then allowed his viral shadow-crafting powers to flow into it. Instantly, the leaves began to lose their rich, green color. They faded to a sickly gray, then crumbled to the ground, leaving the tree a lifeless skeleton. It would stand there forever, but never grow another inch.

"How do you like that, Oracle?!" Herobrine shouted to the night. "You can keep watching, but make no mistake: after I destroy the blacksmith, I'll turn my monsters upon you. You, too, will beg for mercy at my feet, and you'll receive just as much as the blacksmith: none." He stepped out of the forest and faced Olympus Mons. "You can be certain, I'm coming for you both. Soon you will meet your end."

Herobrine's eyes grew brighter and brighter as his rage built to the point of exploding.

"Erebus!" he screamed. "Get ready to attack!"

CHAPTER 26

TO THE NETHER

ameknight moved through the tunnels that wove their way through Olympus Mons like arteries through the body of a rocky giant. He'd remembered them from the last time he'd been to this mountain. It seemed like a million years ago when he'd been here with his friends; but actually, it hadn't happened yet; it was still a hundred years in the future.

He made his way up a tunnel to led to the surface, specifically to the edge of the crater his TNT had made when they'd destroyed Herobrine's small army. Around the mountain were the sounds of zombies, spiders, skeletons, Endermen, and ghasts. Herobrine had surrounded the mountain so none could escape across the surface of the mountain, but he hadn't blocked *all* avenues.

Gameknight smiled.

Glancing up to the sky, he saw softly glowing orange clouds overhead. They had infected everything as far as the eye could see, tiny orange embers now sparkling along the edges of all the misty blocks. It looked like a subtle firework show was going on in the heavens, the glowing embers floating through the air and disappearing before they ever hit the ground.

"This is bad," Gameknight said to himself. "We must stop him."

"Oink," a low voice said next to his feet.

The User-that-is-not-a-user glanced down and found Wilbur at his side.

"Wilbur, you were supposed to wait in the tunnel for me," Gameknight said, a scowl creasing his face.

"Oink, oink," the pig replied defiantly.

The User-that-is-not-a-user smiled. Wilbur was a good friend, and he was here because the pig could likely sense the fear that filled Gameknight's soul. He reached down and patted his friend on his soft pink head.

"Okay, you ready to do this?"

"OINK!"

"Get ready to run fast," Gameknight warned.

Stepping up to the edge of the crater, he moved out into the open and pulled a torch out from his inventory. He then took the biggest breath he could and yelled as loud as he'd ever yelled in his life.

"HEROBRINE, COME GET ME IF YOU'RE NOT AFRAID!"

He planted the torch in the ground, then turned and ran across the crater. As he shot back underground, into the tunnels, he paused for just an instant to place a sign near the tunnel entrance. The sign read: "GK WAS HERE." In the back of his mind, he knew the sign would be important a hundred years in the future.

The two companions dashed through the tunnels, running as fast as their feet would carry them.

Soon, he heard the chuckling sounds of Endermen as they materialized on the side of the mountain where he'd just been. The faint sorrowful moans of zombies could be heard trickling through the stone passage, the clattering of bone and clicking of mandibles adding a rhythmical beat; Herobrine's army had found the entrance. This motivated the pair to run even faster.

They shot through the rocky corridors, heading ever deeper into the bowels of the mountain. As he ran, Gameknight removed the torches marking their path, which would force Herobrine and his monsters to blindly search for him, rather than just follow the trail he'd left behind. And that would give the villagers more time to prepare for the mob's arrival.

Deeper and deeper they went, taking tunnels that sloped downward at a steep angle, the passage resembling a stairway. Eventually, they reached their destination: a gigantic cavern. Gameknight recognized it instantly when they had first found it. This was the place where Herobrine had set up his command blocks, in an attempt to dump lava across all the villages in the Overworld. The User-that-is-not-a-user and his friends had stopped his plot, and destroyed two of the virus's monster kings at the same time.

Gameknight ran into the chamber and headed straight for the ring of obsidian that sat in the center. A sheet of purple light filled the dark rectangle, undulating and pulsing as if it were alive, splashing a lavender glow upon the stone floor that stretched across the cavern; it was a portal to the Nether.

Standing next to it were Carver and Baker. As Gameknight's footsteps echoed through the cave, the two NPCs looked at him and smiled.

"Did he take the bait?" Carver asked.

"Absolutely," the User-that-is-not-a-user said. "It'll take them a while to find this cave, but rest assured . . . they *will* find it."

"Okay," Baker replied. "Fencer just came back and said he found the perfect place for the ambush."

"Great. Then let's go," Gameknight said.

He stepped into the glowing portal. Instantly, his sight began to waver as everything was shaded with a purple hue. And, for the briefest of moments, he could see the dark cavern around him, but at the same time see rivers of lava flowing across a rusty landscape, a rocky ceiling high overhead. Suddenly, a ferocious heat slammed into him like a sledgehammer.

Gameknight stepped away from the portal and fully into the Nether. Behind him, the loud squeals of his friend filled his ears as Wilbur exited behind him. Gameknight bent down and picked up his friend.

"Don't worry, Wilbur. When you get used to the heat, it won't be that bad," Gameknight said.

Baker and Carver then stepped out of the sparkling gateway. Baker's cheeks were flushed as if she were embarrassed; was it from the intense heat of the Nether? Carver, however, had a satisfied grin on his face, like he'd just won some great contest. Gameknight flashed him a questioning glance. The big NPC just shrugged as Baker walked past, then followed her down the reddish-brown hill.

All around him, rust-colored netherrack covered the ground. It had a texture similar to gravel, its grains filled with reds and oranges and browns. Occasionally, brown soul-sand could be seen; Gameknight had warned all the villagers to stay far away from it. Countless rivers of lava criss-crossed the terrain, some fell from the ceiling and formed wide pools of boiling stone, while others spewed out of the side of a hill or jagged wall. But no matter where it came from, all of the lava flowed downhill, toward a great ocean of molten rock. The size of that body of boiling stone always shocked Gameknight when he saw it. In the future, he knew there would be a great fortress on the shore of that ocean, built by slaves taken from the Overworld; his friend Stitcher had been one. The terrifying structure would stretch out across the landscape like a lethal spider waiting to pounce. But now, in the past, the Nether fortress didn't exist.

"Are you coming?" Carver yelled from the bottom of the hill.

"Oh . . . yeah," Gameknight replied.

He ran down the hill with Wilbur bouncing in his arms. The pig had stopped squealing, but was still uncomfortable—they all were.

Stuck to the walls and ceilings were yellow clusters of glowstone, the shining cubes adding a touch of yellow to the orange coming from all the lava. Smoke and ash drifted through the air, making the glowstone difficult to see in the distance, and Gameknight knew it would get even worse when they neared the ocean below.

They all ran downhill, carefully dodging burning cubes of netherrack and pools of boiling rock. At places they had to leap over thin rivers of lava; the heat coming up off those glowing streams was terrible. In this section of the Nether, the landscape was formed of thick layers, each sitting about twenty blocks above the next, forming a terraced structure. Lava spilled down the layers, falling from one level to the next as if it were oozing down a set of giant stairs.

Gameknight smiled; this terrain was perfect. The layers were separated enough to give them room to fight, but still restricted enough to keep the ghasts close to the ground.

When they finally reached the plains that stretched out to the boiling shoreline, Carver led them around a massive hill of Nether quartz. The white crystals in the Nether quartz stood out in shining contrast to the surrounding red nether-rack. It was the only thing in this land of smoke and flame that was not the colors of fire: red, orange, yellow, and sooty brown.

On the other side of the hill, Gameknight found a massive cavern. Well, it wasn't really a cavern, as it had no walls to the left or right, just a ceil-ing. Another layer of netherrack stood above the ground level, at least twenty blocks high. Small clumps of glowstone were clustered sporadically, providing some light but not much. Along one wall was a set of furnaces, each with a flame burning bright inside it. NPCs worked the furnaces, pull-ing out blocks of stone and replacing them with cobblestone and coal. Across the ground, the stone was being used to replace the netherrack, a thin stone pressure plate positioned on the gray cube. The texture of the pressure plate exactly matched the stone cube, making it nearly invisible; they'll be impossible to spot in the gloomy light. Lines of red-stone ran under the netherrack in a complex series of circuits that led to a wall of dispensers hidden in the darkness.

Gameknight could see their plan was shaping up. It had been his initial idea to bring Herobrine and his army—especially the ghasts—down into the Nether, but other villagers had suggested the dispensers and pressure plates. In the end, it was a battle plan that had been formulated by everyone, and many NPCs had contributed ideas that Gameknight would have never considered himself. With everyone working together, it felt like it took some of the responsibility off his shoulders.

Suddenly, a cat-like cry filled the air.

"The ghasts are coming!" Fencer shouted. "Everyone finish up and get to position."

The villagers moved faster, placing more blocks and digging up more netherrack. They reminded the User-that-is-not-a-user of a colony of angry ants. Peering into the darkness under the overhang, Gameknight saw a group of oddly shaped people standing off to the side: the light-crafters. He ran toward them, where he found the Oracle talking to Wolfbrin, the new light-crafter speaking in a growling voice.

"Will you be able to help during the battle?" Gameknight asked, interrupting the conversation. "I think we'll need the assistance."

"We will try, child. Villagers are placing blocks of dirt and sand on the ground as we speak," the Oracle said in a scratchy, aged voice. "But I don't know how well their powers will work down here in this terrible place." She moved closer to Gameknight and spoke in a whisper, for his ears only. "You know, if this plan doesn't work, Herobrine will have you trapped down here."

"If this doesn't work, then it really doesn't matter where we are," he replied. "Herobrine will have the Overworld covered with his infected clouds, with an army of ghasts raining fireballs down onto the villages. He'll be able to wipe out all the NPCs with a single stroke. If this doesn't work, then villagers may become extinct."

The feline yowls grew louder, and now they had with them the sorrowful moans of zombies and the clattering of skeleton bones. Herobrine was getting closer.

"When this is all over, whether we win or lose, you need to go into hiding," Gameknight said. "The spider queen will hunt you across all the biomes of the Overworld, and I fear that if she finds you, it will not end well."

"Thank you for your concern, child, but I think I'll be okay."

"You *must* promise me: when this is over, you go hide."

"Perhaps, but let us see how the day ends before we make plans for the next hundred years."

The Oracle reached out and placed a wrinkled hand on Gameknight's arm. Instantly there was a calming presence in his mind; it was the music of Minecraft. It allowed him to put aside the fear that had been building up since the battle of Olympus Mons, and it felt good to release that stress.

"Now go do your sword thing," the Oracle said. "My light-crafters will be back here, doing what we can."

Gameknight gave her a nod, then looked up at the tall Wolfbrin.

"I have a friend that would love to meet you," the User-that-is-not-a-user said. "He loves your wolves more than anything else, and cares for them as if they were his own children. But sadly, he won't be born for about a century."

"Grrrreat," Wolfbrin said. "Perhaps you can give him my grrrratitude. It'll be a grrrrand adventure today. Maybe I'll still be around when he is borrrrn."

"I hope so," Gameknight replied, then moved to take his position.

Walking carefully past the pressure plates, the User-that-is-not-a-user moved out from under the netherrack overhang. Dispensers studded the ceiling as well as the walls; hopefully they would not be seen until it was too late. Gameknight walked out into the open and moved to the shore-line of the great lava ocean. Waves of heat and ash wafted from the huge body of boiling stone, causing tiny square beads of sweat to form on his brow. Turning, he looked up the hill they'd descended. Their portal was up there, some-where, and likely Herobrine had used it to follow them.

Suddenly, he felt something rubbing against his leg. Looking down, he found Wilbur standing next to him, his pink face staring up at him.

"Oink, oink," Wilbur said in a strong, confident voice.

"I'm glad you feel so brave," the User-that-is-not-a-user said. "But I'm terrified."

"Oink."

"Yeah, I know we don't have much choice. Are you ready?"

The tiny animal rubbed against his leg.

"Okay, here goes," Gameknight said, then drew in a huge breath and shouted as loud as he could. "HEROBRINE, YOU'RE A COWARD AND SHOULD RUN AWAY WHILE YOU HAVE THE CHANCE." He took another breath. "I PITY YOU AND YOUR PATHETIC ARMY!"

An angry scream sliced through the Nether. It was filled with such venomous hatred that it caused tiny square goosebumps to form down Gameknight's spine.

"I think I got his attention," the User-that-is-not-a-user said, gulping.

"Oink, oink," Wilbur replied.

"Come on."

Gameknight turned and ran, just as a fireball streaked through the sky and landed in the lava ocean nearby.

"They're coming!" Gameknight shouted. "And I don't think Herobrine is very happy."

Some of the villagers laughed while others simply repeated the phrase that more and more of the NPCs were using: "Smithy be crazy."

Gameknight drew his diamond sword with his right hand, then grabbed his iron with his left, and waited for Herobrine and his army to crash down upon them.

CHAPTER 27

RAIN OF FIRE

Archers ran out to face up the hill where Herobrine's army was descending from. They fired arrows indiscriminately at the approaching monsters, just to give the impression they were trying to hold them back. But the truth of the matter was that they *wanted* the monster army to come much, much closer.

Gameknight could see fireballs streaking past the opening to their little underground surprise. A rainstorm of fire was raging out on the netherrack plain, but the User-that-is-not-a-user knew the archers would be okay. The NPCs had spotters telling them where the fireballs would hit, and the warriors were safely moving out of the way.

Gameknight knew there were three things you needed to know about ghasts' fireballs:

1. They were terrifying when they were heading straight at you.
2. If they hit you, they did a lot of damage, especially if there was no water nearby.

3. They were easy to avoid.

Gameknight had recently taught the villagers that third truth when they came into the Nether (all of the warriors already knew about the first and second truths). Now the archers were putting their newfound knowledge to the test.

"Move, it's coming right at you," someone yelled.

"Look out," cried another.

Exploding fireballs, cat-like cries, and the shouts of villagers filled the air. Gameknight wanted to run out and help, but he knew he had to stay back. The archers knew what they were doing, and he had to let them do their jobs.

Suddenly, the NPCs ran down the hill and sprinted under the overhang, and he saw some had scorched iron armor with smoldering edges; apparently, the fireballs weren't as easy to avoid as Gameknight had assumed. If they had been in the Overworld, they would have wanted to jump into pools of water to quell the heat from the blasted armor, but it was impossible to place water in the Nether; it evaporated instantly.

"They're coming," Fencer said as he patted the sleeve of his smock, which was burning slightly. He'd been one of the archers out there. "No question about it, they know we're here and they're really mad."

"Great!" Gameknight exclaimed. "Everyone to their positions . . . Archers, get in your holes . . . Villagers, get to your levers. We have only one shot at this, so it must work."

"What are *you* gonna do during all this?" Fencer asked.

"Me?" Gameknight said with a nervous smile. "I'm still the bait."

"Everyone get ready," Carver yelled. "They're coming."

Groups of four climbed into holes in the ground, each hidden in the shadows of the overhang; one warrior with a sword, and the other three with bow and arrows. Others climbed up the walls and took their places next to levers connected to redstone circuits. But the bulk of the army gathered at the back of the chamber, waiting. Only Gameknight stood out in the open, standing directly on a block of glowstone so that all the monsters would see him.

Moans and clicks and clattering bones filled the area. The monsters gathered near the edge of the lava ocean, their hateful eyes all focused on Gameknight999. Smashing his diamond sword on the netherrack around him, the User-that-is-not-a-user made a banging sound that resonated through the rusty stone landscape.

"Where are your cowardly ghasts, Herobrine?" Gameknight shouted. "I want to punish them first for destroying some villages. Then I'll deal with you."

An evil presence materialized at the front of the monster army. He was clad in all black, and had a vile, malicious expression on his face, his two eyes glowing bright with hatred.

"You want to meet my ghasts?" Herobrine shouted. "Very well."

He motioned with one hand, and a group of ghasts floated out of the shadows toward Gameknight999. Balls of fire began to form under the creatures, growing hotter and hotter. Then the evil floating monsters sucked the spheres of flame into their bodies and spit them directly at him.

Rolling to the side, Gameknight easily avoided the attack, then drew his bow and fired. His arrow struck the lead ghast, making it flash red. But instead of firing another shot, he turned and ran to the shadows.

"You see, the blacksmith is already retreating," Herobrine said. "I told you he was a coward." The virus laughed. "Remember, Smithy is mine." His eyes grew brighter. "Monsters . . . ATTACK."

A hundred creatures surged forward, including the ghasts, which floated up near the rough-hewn ceiling. The Endermen stayed near the rear, unable to join the first wave of fighters, while zombies moaned and wailed near the front of the assault. Gameknight watched the wave of fangs and claws approach and was petrified with fear. With all the spiders, zombies, skeletons, ghasts, and Endermen, it was likely the single most vicious army every assembled in Minecraft. Gameknight steadied his shaking hands, remembering the one job he had to do, and moved back out into the open again, so the monsters could see him. The spiders clicked louder as cat-like cries came from the ghasts.

They were getting closer. Gameknight could smell the repulsive, decaying odor that always hovered around zombies like a perpetual cloud of putrid stench. He could hear the spiders that climbed along the ceiling, their claws making a scratching sound as they dug into the netherrack ceiling. The ground began to shake with thunder as the pounding monster feet grew closer.

An arrow zipped past his head; an overeager skeleton had taken a shot at him, but likely had been bumped by another monster nearby, causing the shot to miss. A roar sounded overhead, followed by a fireball that descended onto the offending skeleton. A section of the cave lit up with flickering yellow light as the flames consumed the skeleton's XP.

"The Maker said to save the blacksmith for him!" Malacoda bellowed from far back in the formation. "Destroy the villagers when you find them, but save Smithy for the end. Or ELSE!"

Gameknight gripped his swords tighter and waited, fear and uncertainty growing within.

What if this doesn't work? he thought. *What if the traps don't stop the monsters?*

But everything was happening too quickly for Gameknight to be lost in thought. The first of the spiders stepped forward, reaching a pressure plate camouflaged on top of a block of stone. Lines of redstone powder grew bright as the glowing signals ran to the dispensers, triggering the arrows, which shot out of dark holes in the gray cubes, streaking into the side of the attacking force. Zombies and skeletons screamed out as they flashed red with damage, and the clicking of the spiders grew frantic. Ghasts turned to fire toward the source of the arrows, but their fireballs harmlessly smashed into the wall of stone-lined dispensers.

Instead of retreating, the monsters decided to surge forward, moving as fast as possible across the pressure plates. More arrows were triggered, sending them flying into the vile creatures, but their onslaught never wavered. With so much hatred stored up in the monsters, and so many of them attacking, nothing short of total defeat would stop these creatures.

Skeletons and ghasts fired into the darkness, hoping to hit something, but the only thing visible was Gameknight999. As they drew closer,

Gameknight glanced into the shadows to his right and nodded his head. The thundering voice of Carver suddenly filled the Nether.

"ARCHERS, ATTACK!"

Groups of four suddenly stood from holes in the netherrack. Three archers fired their bows while a fourth villager helped direct their fire. The trio of archers worked together, all firing at the same ghast. With the three arrows striking the beast simultaneously, its HP was immediately consumed. One by one, the square creatures screamed like terrified babies, flashing red, then tilted to the side and disappeared.

Continuing to fire, the archers shot at the ghasts while the monsters continued their advance across the pressure plates. The first wave eventually broke through and they reached the archers. That was when swordsmen leapt out of the shadows, offering a distraction so that the bowmen could climb out of their holes and retreat.

With arrows continuing to streak up at them, the ghasts tried to rise higher into the air, but the netherrack ceiling kept them trapped and within range of the villagers' bows. Their only choice was to retreat, but as the floating giants tried to drift out of the chamber, Malacoda roared with fury.

"Attack, you fools, don't retreat!" the king of the ghasts bellowed.

The floating monsters turned and moved forward, trying to zigzag to make it difficult for the archers to aim.

With the archers pulled back, the rest of the army emerged from the shadows behind Gameknight999, their weapons and armor gleaming in the light from nearby glowstones.

"This battle is boring me!" Gameknight shouted. "Are none of you brave enough to come forward, or are all of you just as cowardly as your late zombie king, Vo-Lok?" He took a step forward. "He begged for mercy at my feet. But I laughed at him, just like I'm laughing at you know. Then I destroyed him."

The zombies growled in rage. They all knew about the demise of their king at the hands of the village's blacksmith leader. Surging forward, they pushed the rest of the monster army ahead with them in one giant mass.

Gameknight smiled, then turned and ran to the line of villagers behind him. As he sprinted, he nodded his head, giving the second signal. NPCs hiding in the ceiling set redstone torches to more dispensers, activating the devices and causing them to shoot out blinking cubes of TNT, courtesy of TNTbrin. The red-and-white-striped cubes fell amongst the monsters, and went unnoticed . . . at first.

But then . . . *BOOM!*

The first of the blocks exploded, tearing huge chunks out of the netherrack floor as balls of fire blossomed into life. Then more of the striped cubes detonated, punctuating the growls and moans and clattering of the monsters with thunderous blasts of destruction.

Monsters ran in all directions, trying to avoid the devastation, but the dispensers were everywhere. Ghasts launched their fireballs up at the ceiling, trying to contain the attacking villagers they believe were hidden overhead. The spheres of flaming death smashed into the dispensers and raised walkways, casting wide circles of light on the surroundings. That was when the monsters saw that the villagers in the ceiling had already fled. The ghasts cried out in frustration, then turned their rage back toward Gameknight999 and the other villagers.

Fireballs fell down upon the NPCs like a fiery rain. But this time, the villagers stood in pairs, each with their swords held at the ready. With the zombies, skeletons, and spiders busy with the TNT falling on their heads, the defenders were able to concentrate mostly on balls of fire streaking toward them from the ghasts. They batted the fireballs away with their swords, sending some of them far to the side, and even sending them careening back right to their source. Ghasts cried out in shock and pain as the burning spheres they'd fired moments before ended up crashing back into them, scorching HP into ash.

The floating monsters fell by the dozens as their own attacks came back to foil them.

Archers fired in groups of four again, one NPC directing the trio of attackers as well as defending them with their sword. Arrows and fireballs flew back and forth until finally, the ceiling was clear of ghasts; they'd all been destroyed.

The dispensers in the ceiling had exhausted their supply of TNT, as had the wall of dispensers firing the arrows. What was left of the monster army was pathetic; a mere shadow of itself. But the villagers showed no sign of letting up.

"Everyone, ATTACK!" Gameknight yelled.

"Smithy be crazy!" the villagers replied as they charged at the remnant of Herobrine's army.

They smashed into the surviving monsters, with Gameknight999 acting as the point of the spear. Spider and zombie claws met iron swords as skeleton and NPC arrows flew back and forth like angry, pointed insects. But the skeleton arrows were grossly outnumbered.

Gameknight was at the center of it all, his diamond sword leaving behind great swaths of destruction followed up by the iron blade in his other hand. Monster after monster fell before him. Nearby, Baker and Carver led a group of armored villagers, tearing into a large group of spiders. The legendary axe tore through dark fuzzy bodies as the Carver of Monsters charged forward. Creatures flashed red as they were thrown aside like ragdolls. Spiders tried to escape the melee, but archers had now built up towers of stone and dirt, and were firing down upon the monsters, ensuring none could flee.

Gameknight spotted Weaver battling with two zombies. He kicked a spider away and moved to his friend's side. Swinging his diamond sword with all his might, he destroyed one of the decaying monsters while Weaver destroyed the other. Then clicking came to them from the right. Turning, Gameknight charged at the spider, blocking a spider claw with his diamond sword, then attacking with his iron. The creature moved backward, its eight eyes glowing bright red with hatred. He could see it was getting ready to leap into the air, but suddenly Wilbur dashed forward and bit one of its fuzzy legs. When the monster looked down in surprise, both Gameknight and Weaver attacked, destroying the rest of its HP in seconds.

"Fencer, take a group of warriors around the left flank!" Gameknight yelled. "Carver, take a squadron to the right. Let's crush them in the center."

The villagers split up and attacked the monsters from three sides. They drove forward, swords slicing through the air and arrows zipping around everywhere. The monsters tried to retreat, but many fell into the massive crater created by the TNT blasts, trapping all the monsters but the spiders. Soon, the only survivors were zombies and skeletons trapped in the huge recession, looking for cover in the deep netherrack hole.

"We did it!" Weaver yelled.

"SMITHY . . . SMITHY . . . SMITHY . . ." the villagers chanted, all cheering with glee.

Though not all celebrated. Gameknight looked about him at all the armor and weapons that floated on the ground. Many had lost their lives in this battle, and their deaths weighed heavily on his mind. But what concerned him more was the ease of that battle. He had expected overwhelming forces, but instead, they faced a force equal in size to their own. That was uncharacteristic of Herobrine. He liked to attack when he had the complete advantage, and in this battle, he hadn't.

Suddenly, maniacal laughter filled the air. At the opening to their underground battlefield, backlit by the bright orange light from the lava ocean, Herobrine stood with eyes glowing bright.

"That was a good warm-up," the evil virus said. "But now that all of your little traps are used up, allow me to introduce you to my *real* army."

A massive group of zombies and skeletons and spiders and Endermen emerged out from behind the vile shadow-crafter. There were hundreds of the monsters, all of them growling and snarling at the villagers. Slowly, Malacoda floated down next to Herobrine as Erebus and Shaikulud moved to their Maker's side. The collection of monsters all glared directly at Gameknight999 with hatred in their eyes.

What do we do? What do we do? Gameknight thought. *How do I come up with a way to stop this gigantic army of monsters?*

Waves of panic spread through him.

The monsters took a step forward, anxious to destroy the blacksmith and all his friends. They were unable to hold back their enthusiasm for destruction.

"I can see you're all excited," Herobrine said. "So please, help yourself . . . ATTACK!"

The monsters charged forward, and all Gameknight999 could do was stand there and watch.

CHAPTER 28

A NEW PLAN

"Smithy, what do we do?" Weaver asked.

Gameknight didn't reply. All he could do was stare at the approaching horde as their fangs and claws glistened in the light from the glowstones overhead.

I don't have any more tricks up my sleeve, he thought. *I've failed.*

Just then, the music of Minecraft flowed across the Nether. It made the monsters stop their charge as they howled in frustration and pain, many of the zombies putting their clawed hands over their decaying ears.

You don't need to do this alone, an ancient voice said in his head. *Accept that you don't have all the answers and ask for help. Showing you don't have all the answers is not a bad thing. It just makes you like everyone else.*

Gameknight glanced at the Oracle standing to the rear of the army, her strange-looking light-crafters grouped protectively around her. He gave her a strained smile, then nodded his head.

"Carver, Baker, Fencer . . . I need your help," Gameknight said. "I don't know how to stop all these monsters so we can then destroy Herobrine. We need to figure this out together." He paused for a moment and looked at his friends with fear in his eyes. "Help me . . . please."

A smile grew on Fencer's face. He slapped Carver on the back, then laughed out loud.

"Ha . . . no problem," Fencer said, and Carver and Baker both sounded their agreement as well.

Quickly, the four friends came up with a plan. Some of the ideas Gameknight would have never considered. But because they worked together, each contributed their own special strength and creativity to the discussion, forming a plan that had plenty of surprises for Herobrine.

Slowly, the music of Minecraft faded, and the monsters could continue their charge.

"Archers, move now!" Fencer shouted as he pulled out his bow and disappeared into the stairways that led up into the ceiling, a third of the army following him.

"Villagers, place dirt on the ground, quickly," Baker said as she slowly backed up, placing blocks of dirt here and there.

A group of NPCs quickly moved across the netherrack surface, depositing blocks of dirt in no particular order, while others dug holes straight down into the ground, two blocks deep. Any zombie or skeleton that fell into the hole would be trapped and effectively taken out of the fight. Small squads of warriors pulled out shovels and began digging long, two-block-deep channels that extended directly away from the approaching horde. The angry moans and hungry growls made the villagers dig faster than they ever thought possible.

When all of their preparations were complete, the fastest amongst them, Fisher, ran toward the monsters with flint and steel in his hands. Sprinting to the edge of the crater that had been carved into the netherrack floor by the TNT, he started to place a line of fire across the edge of the huge crater. Instantly, the netherrack took to flame. Quickly, Fisher ran back to the NPC formation, a smile on his face.

"Now the monsters must pass through the flames in order to get to us," Carver said. "That was a brilliant idea, Baker."

"Well, thanks, I was thinking that if we . . ."

But she was stopped short, as the monsters emerged from the huge crater. Their angry faces were visible through the flames that stood between the opposing side, but to the NPCs' surprise, they didn't even hesitate, and walked through the flames like an unstoppable flood, the front rank pushed forward from behind. Some of the monsters fell on the flames, overwhelmed with damage and pain. They flashed red as their HP was consumed, but their flailing bodies snuffed out some of the fire. After the loss of a few dozen zombies and skeletons, the fires were all but extinguished.

The horde of vicious creatures moved toward them, relentless with their desire for destruction. Some zombies and skeletons fell in the holes in the ground, their bodies suddenly disappearing from view, but the holes were too few to make any real difference.

"Everyone ready?" Gameknight asked.

"SMITHY!" the villagers yelled.

"ATTACK!"

Instead of crashing straight into the mob, the archers all jumped down into the long two-block-deep channels filled with zombies and skeletons. They started shooting along the length of the channel, which was so narrow that the monsters were unable to get out of the way. Arrows struck the first monster until it disappeared with a *pop*, then the one behind it, then the one after. More warriors stood on the edges of the canal and fired down at the row of creatures lined up. Bowstrings hummed the song of battle as twenty warriors fired as fast as they could draw. The zombies and skeletons moaned in fear and pain as they fell under the storm of arrows.

At the same time, the warriors in the walkways above the battlefield fired their pointed rain down upon the mob. Arrow after arrow was released, so many that it almost turned the air black, but even with the monsters being destroyed in the channels and from above, there were just too few bows to slow their advance.

That meant that it was the light-crafters' turn. Clumps of long, snake-like grass began to sprout from blocks of dirt, ensnaring the legs of passing monsters. Large green cacti burst into life, their sharp spines poking into those nearby. Walls of cacti soon stood before the monsters, blocking their progress, but still Herobrine's army did not slow. They ran right into the prickly cactus, then climbed on top of each other until a living bridge was made over the pointy obstacles.

Across the battlefield, the monsters charged through the barbed hail, refusing to slow. They crashed down upon the defenders like a tidal wave of fangs and claws. There were three monsters battling each villager, with even more of the vicious creatures waiting in the wings for their turn to fight. The NPCs fought bravely, but many fell under the onslaught. There were just too few of them; they were completely outnumbered. Gameknight knew he had to do something, fast, or they were finished. And he knew of only one thing that might help.

"HEROBRINE, COME FACE SMITHY IN BATTLE, IF YOU'RE NOT A COWARD!" Gameknight screamed.

The monsters all gasped in surprise and stepped back from the villagers for just a moment.

An icy chill ran down Gameknight's spine as Herobrine materialized right behind his monsters, his eyes glowing bright with excitement.

"Why don't you come out here and let us decide this, just you and me!" the User-that-is-not-a-user challenged.

"My, my, the blacksmith has a little courage after all. Last time we faced each other, you had friends there to protect you. Are you going to hide behind your friends again?"

Gameknight stepped forward and kicked one of the zombies backward so he could face the evil virus. The creature stood and began to attack when Herobrine brought his own swords down on the monster. The creature gave off a sad moan as it disappeared, leaving Herobrine directly facing Gameknight999.

"You don't see any of my friends nearby, do you?"

"No, I don't."

"Then come out here and face me if you're brave enough," Gameknight said. "If you win, these villagers will be your slaves and build your Nether fortress down here on the shores of the lava ocean. But if I defeat you, we'll be given safe passage to the Overworld."

"Smithy, NO!" Carver cried.

Gameknight held his hand up to silence his friend.

"This was how the ending was meant to be, isn't that right, Herobrine?"

"It was inevitable," the evil virus said with a sneer. "Everything that has a beginning has an end, and this is your end, blacksmith."

"We'll see, you failed program," Gameknight growled. "Come on, Herobrine, let's dance."

CHAPTER 29

FRIENDS

Gameknight charged forward. Being from the future, he had the benefit of fighting Herobrine before, and he knew the virus's tricks. But this was the first time Herobrine had ever faced off against Gameknight999, and he didn't realize that his opponent held the tactical advantage.

The User-that-is-not-a-user swung his diamond sword, even though he knew Herobrine would teleport away just in the nick of time. It was a decoy, and just as he swung the diamond sword, he spun around, knowing that Herobrine would materialize right behind him and try to catch him off guard. That was exactly what happened, and Gameknight brought his iron blade up just in time to deflect Herobrine's sword. The razor-sharp weapons smashed together with such strength that it sounded like they were inside a thundercloud.

Herobrine had clearly not expected his foe to anticipate his powers of teleportation, and block his attack. He was caught off guard, and before the evil virus could adjust, Gameknight brought his diamond sword down on the virus's arm. It glanced off Herobrine's armor, ringing like a gong. The virus then disappeared from sight, teleporting to some-place new. Staying low to the ground, the User-that-is-not-a-user turned until he spotted a pair of legs. Leaping high in the air, he brought his sword down and was easily blocked. But before Herobrine could counterattack or teleport away, Gameknight crouched and spun again, this time extending his leg. It struck Herobrine's ankles, taking his feet out from under him. The vile shadow-crafter fell with a thud. Not waiting for him to respond, Gameknight slashed at the Maker's legs, striking them hard and making him flash red with damage.

The monsters around them all gasped as they saw their leader take damage from the blacksmith. Zombies growled and spiders clicked their mandi-bles together in anger.

Gameknight stood, but Herobrine had already disappeared. He turned quickly, looking around for his enemy, but couldn't find him anywhere. It was impossible to think Herobrine had run away; his ego and thirst for destruction would not permit it.

Suddenly, a scream could be heard from over-head. Herobrine had teleported to one of the over-head walkways the villagers had built. He leapt off and fell straight down on top of Gameknight999, knocking him to the ground and sending his iron sword skittering out of reach. Bringing his diamond sword up, Gameknight blocked his enemy's attack, then stood and glanced at the Oracle.

Are they coming? he thought.

Not yet, she replied, the words flashing through his mind. *Keep delaying him.*

Gameknight knew Herobrine and his monsters would never keep their end of the agreement. If he defeated the shadow-crafter, the other monsters would still fall upon them and destroy every villager in the Nether. The User-that-is-not-a-user had to keep them all busy until help arrived, if it came at all.

Rolling sideways, Gameknight charged at his adversary. As usual, Herobrine disappeared, then materialized behind the blacksmith. But instead of turning to block the attack, Gameknight kept moving forward, lunging toward his iron blade that lay on the ground. Stooping, he reached down and grasped the hilt. But as he lifted his arm to bring the sword around, an arrow from a nearby skeleton struck him in the back. Gameknight yelled out in pain, drawing his enemy's gaze.

Herobrine quickly seized on a moment of weakness and teleported right on top of the iron sword, pinning Gameknight's hand under the handle, his fingers painfully pinched. He tried to pull away, but Herobrine was putting too much force down on the weapon; his hand was trapped.

"It seems you're stuck," Herobrine said as he slid his feet along the blade, moving closer. He pointed his own sword directly at Gameknight999's face. "You are beaten, Smithy. Are you ready to beg for mercy?"

"Never!"

The User-that-is-not-a-user glanced at the Oracle. She shook her head.

"That old hag cannot help you, Smithy. I have beaten you, and soon you'll be destroyed." He moved forward and stepped right on Gameknight's hand, causing pain to shoot up his arm. "But first,

I think we'll watch as my spiders destroy that old woman. There's something about her I don't like."

"No, you can't," Gameknight pleaded.

"That is where you're wrong, blacksmith. I can do anything I want. Minecraft is mine. The Overworld is mine. It's all mine!"

"But you still cannot escape," Gameknight spat. "You're trapped here and will never escape. Your pathetic attempts to flee these servers will never work. You're an inept and obsolete piece of code that should be deleted!"

Herobrine's eyes grew bright with rage.

"How dare you speak to Herobrine like that!"

The zombies growled and the skeletons notched arrows to bowstrings, while the villagers did the same. Gameknight glanced at the Oracle and saw an expression of sadness on her old wrinkled face, her eyes cast to the ground in defeat.

Then, suddenly, a sound echoed off the netherrack floor.

"HOOOOOOOOOOWL!" Wolfbrin screamed, his voice like a booming rumble of thunder, filled with strength and pride.

"Shut your pet up," Herobrine growled to the Oracle, but she ignored him.

Another howl floated across the land. It sounded like the echo of Wolfbrin's, but stranger.

"What is this?" Herobrine demanded. "Some kind of sound trick?"

Gameknight tried to pull his hand free from under the sword, but it was still held to the ground. He glanced at Baker and motioned with his head at Herobrine.

"You think that woman will last long against me?" Herobrine said, guffawing. "She wouldn't stand a chance."

"I don't think she should fight you," the User-that-is-not-a-user replied. "I was just thinking she should give you her nice sword."

"What?" Baker asked. "Never!"

Herobrine laughed, his eyes glowing bright as he stared at the shining iron weapon.

"You know," Gameknight added, hoping she might get the hint. "Like Digger."

"Never. I'll never give up my sword!"

"After I destroy your leader here, I'm gonna take her sword and throw it in the lava ocean, just because I can," Herobrine said, laughing.

The dark shadow-crafter raised his iron weapon high in the air, preparing for the blow that would destroy the blacksmith. Baker then stepped forward, heaving her sword in a strong, overhead throw aimed right at Herobrine's chest.

Gameknight watched as time seemed to slow down. Baker's sword tumbled gracefully through the air as Herobrine's blade descended toward his body. It was now a race, sword vs. sword. Which would reach their destination first? Herobrine glanced up just as the spinning weapon struck him in the shoulder. He flashed red with damage. With his eyes flaring bright, the evil virus disappeared at the speed of thought and materialized a few blocks away.

Gameknight leapt up with his iron sword now in his sore hand and his diamond blade held at the ready. Baker stepped to his side and retrieved her own weapon, Carver on her other side.

"Let's get him," Gameknight said in a low voice. "We can't let Herobrine escape."

The trio charged forward, yelling at the top of their lungs. But Herobrine just smiled and disappeared, materializing amongst his monsters.

"I knew the blacksmith was a coward," Herobrine spat. "And now everyone has . . ."

Wolfbrin let out another strong, proud howl, cutting off the evil shadow-crafter's words. The light-crafter's voice echoed in their ears, but louder somehow, as if it were composed of many voices, all proud and strong.

Gameknight glanced at the Oracle, confused.

"Just some friends showing up to the party," the old woman said with a huge grin.

"Friends?" Gameknight asked. And then he understood. "Friends! Herder, I wish you were here right now!"

Suddenly, a wave of furry white creatures flooded onto the battlefield, streaming across the netherrack like bolts of lightning. Hundreds and hundreds of wolves ran toward the monster army, their eyes bright red with rage.

Wolfbrin howled again, then charged forward with hands outstretched, sharp nails glistening in the yellow light from the overhead glow stones.

"Everyone, ATTACK!" Gameknight shouted.

"Smithy be crazy!" many replied as they ran forward.

Gripping his swords firmly in his hands, the User-that-is-not-a-user charged at the enemy, find-ing himself alongside the tall, white-haired light-crafter. They crashed into the zombies, Gameknight slashing with his swords while Wolfbrin carved away with his sharp, claw-like nails. Treebrin then joined them, his big, woody fists smashing into zombies and skeletons, doing terrible damage.

The other villagers now ran forward to join the fight, but many of the vile creatures didn't even notice them approach; they had their backs turned, more afraid of the wolves than they were of the NPCs. The battle was savage and terrible; Minecraft itself seemed to shake at the ferocity, glitching ever so slightly. Many villagers lost their lives, but that was nothing compared to the destruction being brought down upon the monsters.

Wolfbrin laughed as he fought, slashing at a spider here and kicking a skeleton into piles of loose bones there. Gameknight smiled as he battled at the light-crafter's side. Soon, Baker was there as well, doing her graceful dance of death, her sword flashing through the air so fast it was difficult to see. Carver swung his massive axe, tearing into multiple monsters with a single stroke.

The monsters now could see they would soon be defeated and stopped fighting in order to flee. Because of their numbers, the villagers and the wolves could not destroy them all; many escaped out onto the planes of the Nether.

"Follow them," Gameknight yelled. "We must catch Herobrine so we can stop the infection of Minecraft by the ghasts."

The villagers stormed across the battlefield and ran out onto the shores of the great lava ocean. Archers fired on the escaping monsters as the wolves sprinted across the rusty plain, bringing their strong jaws down upon decaying bony legs.

It was chaos across the Nether. Monsters were fleeing in all directions. Herobrine was nowhere to be seen. A huge group of ghasts were descending toward them from the direction of the Nether portal. Archers moved into groups of three as fireballs rained down upon the landscape.

"Everything's out of . . . out of . . . out of control," Gameknight shouted.

The server is glitching, he thought.

"Where's Herobrine?"

"There!" the Oracle said, pointing with her crooked wooden cane.

Far from the battle, Herobrine looked down upon his failed battle, eyes glowing bright white with rage.

"We'll never get him," Gameknight said. "The ghasts will cover the Overworld. We've lost."

What do I do? he thought, hoping from some answer to appear in his head. *What do I do?*

Suddenly, the loudest blast of thunder ever heard in Minecraft boomed through the Nether, followed by an insanely bright crack of lightning that caused everyone to look away and shudder in fear. When they looked back, they saw a single person standing where the lightning had struck, with letters floating in the air, a long silvery threat extending up from their head. Gameknight took a step closer, then another one, until he could read the letters. He gasped in shock. The letters formed the name N O T C H.

CHAPTER 30

NOTCH

Notch glared at the monsters around him, then noticed the villagers in full armor and frowned, clearly confused. He took a step toward one of the zombies. The ghasts and skeletons, unsure what to make of this new arrival, opened fire, launching fireballs and arrows at the stranger. Zombies charged at the newcomer, unsure who he was.

One of the zombies spotted Wilbur and charged at the small pig from behind, striking the pink animal with his claws. Gameknight moved to protect his little friend, slashing at the monster and causing it to disappear as the decaying creature's HP was consumed.

But, by now, Notch was taking serious damage from the ghasts and skeletons, flashing red with damage until he too disappeared, his items falling to the ground.

How could that be? Gameknight thought. *How could a few zombies and skeletons defeat the mighty*

Notch, the creator of Minecraft? It didn't make any sense.

"Who was that?" one of the villagers asked.

But before the User-that-is-not-a-user could answer, Notch reappeared. But instead of just standing there on the ground, opening himself up for further attacks, he floated up into the air. Gameknight realized that the programmer of Minecraft was now in creative mode, and he looked mad.

"You like shooting at people, do you?" he yelled, his voice echoing off the netherrack walls.

He paused for a moment as if he were doing something else, then suddenly bolts of lightning came down from the rocky ceiling, striking the ghasts and skeletons. Gameknight could see the jagged, white-hot energy tearing into the ghasts' skin, leaving deep scars. The skeletons that were hit seemed to almost catch fire, as if barely visible flames were licking at their bones. Quickly, the bony monsters charred, their pale, white extremities now an ashen black.

"Minecraft is supposed to be a place of creativity and discovery, not battles and violence," Notch yelled. "I made Minecraft for people to come together, not attack one another. This is all wrong."

One of the ghasts gave off an evil feline cry. It drew Notch's attention.

"If you ghasts love your fireballs so much, then I'll make sure that you forever stay down here in the Nether. I have scarred your faces so that all will know your vile nature, and tears of regret for your misdeeds will be dropped to the ground upon your death."

He turned to the skeletons that lay strewn on the ground, some of them making an effort to stand again.

"The skeletons before me will also be sentenced to an eternity in the Nether. May your charred bones remind you, forever, of your violent actions."

"Oink," Wilbur said as he rubbed against Gameknight's leg.

One of the zombies growled and reached out to the harmless pink animal. Before the monster could grasp Wilbur with its claws, bolts of lightning stabbed down at it. Howls of pain and fear came from all the zombies as sheets of lightning struck the decaying monsters. But then, the strangest thing of all happened; their moans and growls developed a squeal-like sound to them. As the bright-white light faded, the zombies now had a new, pink side to them, and their shirts were shredded, revealing bony ribs sticking out from one side.

"You want to kill an innocent pig? I don't think so," Notch said. "As punishment, you zombies will forever be half-monster and half-pig. You'll be zombie pigmen, and will always search the Nether for that which will change you back into a zombie, though you'll never find it. Now BEGONE!"

The newly formed zombie pigmen, complete with gold swords and shining golden armor, began to shuffle off, walking aimlessly, oblivious of everyone around them as they sought the cure to their existence that would never be found.

Notch then floated toward Gameknight and the villagers. As he approached, Gameknight searched the sea of faces, looking for Weaver.

"Weaver, where are you?" Gameknight asked. "Fencer, where is Weaver?"

The villager shook his head. "I saw him on the edge of the battle, but then I lost sight of him."

Gameknight scanned the villagers frantically, looking for the young boy. Then he noticed something near the edge of the Great Lava Ocean. It was clearly a portal, but instead of obsidian, it was made of diamond blocks, a shimmering silvery film undulating across the center.

What kind of portal is that? Gameknight thought.

Suddenly, Notch spoke again.

"You NPCs shouldn't be here," he said.

The villagers just stood there in shock, unsure of who this person was or what to say, until finally Fencer broke the silence.

"Who are you?" he asked.

"I am Notch, the creator of Minecraft."

Instantly, all the villagers knelt and lowered their heads, except for Gameknight999. Notch glanced at the villagers before him, their weapons and armor shining in the orange light of the Nether.

"Why are all my villagers armed?" Notch asked. "Minecraft is supposed to be peaceful. I did not program wars to be fought between villagers and monsters."

None of the villagers spoke. They were all clearly terrified by the user floating in the air before them.

"Excuse me, but Notch, this has all happened because of Herobrine," Gameknight said. "He is the virus that has infected Minecraft, and he escaped our attempts to catch and destroy him."

The Oracle walked up next to Gameknight and stared up at the programmer.

"I am the anti-virus program you created to stop the virus," the old woman said in a scratchy voice.

"Herobrine has done something both wonderful and terrible. He's altered Minecraft forever, causing these villagers and myself to become alive."

"Alive?" Notch said. "How can that be?"

"He was programmed with artificial intelligence software," Gameknight explained. "And when he—"

"Of course, he interacted with my own artificial intelligence code," Notch said as he put the pieces of the puzzle together in his head. "So all of you are alive?"

Gameknight nodded, remembering that he couldn't reveal himself as the User-that-is-not-a-user, but the rest of the villagers stayed on their knees, looking to the ground.

"Stand up, all of you," Notch demanded. "You look foolish."

The villagers stood and faced their programmer, reverent awe covering all of their square faces, all except for Gameknight999. He knew Notch was just a man, a user like himself.

"You villagers should not be here in the Nether," Notch said. "You should not be using weapons and should not be fighting monsters. This was not what I intended. I saw fortifications around many of your villages, and some of them were even completely destroyed. I don't like this. Everything needs to be reset back the way it was, with your hands linked across your chests. You'll have no need for weapons and armor. Whatever damage this Herobrine has caused will be undone."

Bolts of lightning began stabbing down from the rocky ceiling.

"Fencer, you have to find Weaver," Gameknight said quickly. "He was right next to me, then he disappeared."

More lightning fell down upon the villagers, and one by one it carried them each away, back to their villages with their status reset and arms linked across their chests.

"I saw him by that diamond portal down there," Fencer said, "but now I don't see him. . . ."

Suddenly, a bolt of lightning struck Fencer, transporting him back to his village, back home. Eventually, all of the villagers had vanished from the Nether, leaving only the Oracle, her light-crafters, and Gameknight999 behind. A bolt of lightning fell from the sky and struck the User-that-is-not-a-user, but when the harsh light faded, he was still standing there.

Notch drifted closer.

"Why didn't you disappear?" Notch asked.

Gameknight reached up and removed his helmet.

"You aren't a villager—you're a user!"

The User-that-is-not-a-user nodded his head.

"You need to know," Gameknight explained, "Herobrine is planning on covering the Overworld with his ghasts. He's infecting the clouds so they all spawn the evil creatures. If they. . . ."

"Don't worry, I've reset the clouds. The Overworld has been reset. All is as it should be. The zombies and skeletons will fear the sun forever. I was considering altering their code to let them move freely about the land, but I can see the destruction they are capable of. So, I have created zombie-towns and skeleton-towns for them, complete with HP fountains. They'll not wander far from their underground prisons, and they'll never see the clear blue sky again. That will be their punishment for their transgressions."

"What of the Endermen?" the Oracle asked.

Notch laughed.

"Yes, the Endermen . . .that was a clever creation by the virus. I'll allow them to live, but they'll be banished to a new land that I just added to Minecraft, called The End. It'll be a desolate place that will remind them to be a source of good rather than evil. There they'll find a little pet of mine that will watch over them on their floating island. These dark creatures will never again know the joy of cleansing themselves in water. Instead, I have made water to be like acid to them. It will burn their skin and remind them of the evil deeds that led them to this end."

He smiled, then turned to Gameknight999.

"As for you, how did you get here? I haven't even opened up Minecraft to users yet."

"It's a long story," Gameknight replied with a shrug.

"First that virus got in, and now you," Notch growled. "Did my anti-virus program even work at all?"

"Of course she did," Gameknight replied quickly, defending his friend, the Oracle.

Notch raised a hand, silencing him.

"I can see that the spiders hunt you," the Minecraft programmer said to the Oracle. "You must hide from them for a while, for I cannot protect you unless I am in Minecraft."

"It's alright," the old woman replied. "I've created wolves to hunt Herobrine, and I can watch his movements through the leaves of the trees. I'll continue the fight to stop the virus, though I fear it'll take more time."

"Understood. I have prepared a jungle temple for you," Notch said, "where there will be room for your wolves and light-crafters as well. The spiders will not be able to enter; you'll be safe there."

"Thank you, my programmer," she replied.

"Good hunting," Notch said.

More bolts of lightning struck the ground, hitting the Oracle and all of her light-crafters and wolves, causing them to disappear, leaving the two users alone.

"Now for you," Notch said as he turned to face Gameknight999. "I need to understand how you hacked into my server, and I want to know your name, right now."

Suddenly, a stream of words began to flow through his mind. Someone from the physical world was typing to him in the chat.

Tommy, I told you not to use the digitizer in the storm, his father typed in chat. *It's time to leave. Say good-bye to Crafter and all your friends.*

He glanced up at Notch and spoke quickly. "My name is—"

But before he could complete the sentence, a circle of light enveloped Gameknight999. Fingers of heat and freezing cold kneaded his body as the Gateway of Light pulled him from the digital realm and back into the real world. And as the sphere of light became brighter and brighter, the last thing Gameknight saw was the confused look on Notch's face . . . and then everything went black.

CHAPTER 31

THE PROPHECY

Tommy woke with a splitting headache. Usually it was because when the Digitizer knocked him out, he had a tendency to hit his head on the desk. But this time it was different. The trip from the distant past in Minecraft to the physical world had taken a larger toll on him; the hots hotter and the colds even colder. It was as if the Digitizer had difficulty bringing him back, maybe because he was farther away in time. Maybe adding a time warp to the trip from the digital to the physical was a strain on the electronics.

"Son," a stern voice said from behind him.

Tommy sat up, wiped the drool from his chin, and turned to face his father.

"Hi, Dad," Tommy said with a smile.

"I told you not to use the Digitizer in the storm and you did it anyway." A scowl crossed his father's bearded face. "Next time, when I say. . . ."

His dad stopped speaking and pointed at the computer screen. Usually, when they came back into the physical world, the image on the screen was frozen, but this time, they could see villagers moving about. Baker, Carver, Fencer, and all the other villagers all in Smithy's village were walking across the grassy plains. They looked so peaceful with their arms linked across their chests, hands buried in opposite sleeves.

But then Tommy realized that he was still logged in, somehow.

"Wait, I have to do one more thing."

"Tommy, don't you think you've done enough? It's time to stop."

"I will in just a minute."

Tommy pulled his wireless keyboard closer and grabbed his mouse. He typed */gamemode 1* and put himself in creative mode. Opening his inventory, he quickly pulled out two books and placed them in his hot bar, then opened the first book and typed as fast as he could:

A time will come in the distant future when a stranger from a strange land will come to Minecraft. The appearance of the User-that-is-not-a-user will signify the beginning of the final battle for the Source and for all life. If the User-that-is-not-a-user fails in his quest, then all life will be extinguished on these electronic worlds. The Gateway of Light will then allow the mobs, with their hatred and malice toward all living things, to enter into the physical world, where they will bathe themselves in death and destruction, until all life is exterminated.

He signed the book with the words *The Prophecy*. When he looked at it in his inventory, he found the title, but the author's name was blank . . . perfect. Opening the second book, he typed:

Creatures of the Nether will try to form a ring of diamond-crafting benches. If they are allowed to do this, then they will create a portal that will take these evil monsters directly to the Source. These diamond-crafting benches can only be made by full-fledged crafters. When a circle of twelve is formed with a thirteenth at their center, the portal will activate. It will give the monsters of the Overworld and the creatures of the Nether access to the Source. This must not be allowed, for all life will hang by the thinnest of threads, and only strength, courage, and faith in your friends will prevent the violent monsters from destroying everything.

Tommy sighed. He opened his inventory again and found a potion of invisibility. After drinking it, he saw gray swirls floating up into his field of view on the 1080p monitor; he knew that for what he was about to do, he couldn't be seen.

Slowly, he hit double space and flew up into the air, then glided to the village, the landscape scrolling smoothly on the screen. He found Carver and Baker in one of the houses, talking quietly. Tommy couldn't hear anything they were saying. In fact, he couldn't hear anything. Likely it was because he didn't have the speakers turned on—but it didn't matter. Floating over Baker, he dropped one of the books. It landed in her inventory. He then floated over Carver and threw the other one into the big NPCs hands.

They both noticed that something happened and looked around, but obviously saw nothing.

"They'll find the books soon enough," Tommy said to his monitor.

"What are you doing?" his father asked.

"You won't believe it when I tell you, but first, I have one more thing to do."

He flew out of the house, then streaked across the village, looking for Weaver. Instantly, Tommy noticed the fortified wall was gone, as were the archer towers. But the tall cobblestone watch-tower was still present; Notch must have liked that addition.

Soaring over the community like an invisible bird, he went into every house and down into the crafting chamber and into the forest nearby, but saw no trace of Weaver.

"Tommy, it's time to turn it off," his father said. "I think you have some explaining to do."

"I know, I can't wait to tell you what happened, Dad, but first I have to find. . . ."

"I'm sure your friends are all right, but for now, it's time to switch it off. There are more days ahead for Minecraft. Right now, it's late and time for bed. And we can discuss the fact that you ignored what I said about the Digitizer tomorrow morning."

"Awwww."

Tommy wanted to resist, but he could tell from his dad's voice that it would do no good. He looked at his Minecraft friends from the distant past one last time, somehow knowing that when he returned to the game he wouldn't be able to access the game's past again, then logged out and turned off the computer.

"Come on, son, it's time for bed," his dad said. "Maybe you'll dream of three-headed dragons and fortified villagers and strange new distant worlds in Minecraft."

"Maybe," Tommy said, then turned away from the computer as he thought about his new friends, a smile on his face.

MINECRAFT SEEDS

These Minecraft seeds were tested for version 1.9. I had some difficulty finding anything in the normal places online as 1.9 disappeared quickly and became 1.10. So I just created a world and looked around until I found the following things. Sorry they are so far apart, but in creative mode, you can fly to these easily enough.

You'll find all of these things much easier on the Gameknight999 Minecraft server. The IP address is mc.gameknight999.com. Use */warp bookwarps* on the survival server and you'll find the secret path to the BookWarp room. Just click the button and get

teleported to see that terrain or structure. I hope you enjoy these bookwarps.

Chapter 3 – Desert well:
    5933130188688503680
    x: -1915, y: 69, z: -1291

Chapter 5 – Savanna village:
    5933130188688503680
    x: -1713, y: 70, z: -788

Chapter 13 – Mega Taiga:
    5933130188688503680
    x: -4021, y: 74, z: -860

Chapter 16 – Waterfalls:
    On Gameknight999 Minecraft Server

Chapter 19 – Desert temple:
    5933130188688503680
    x: -4021, y: 74, z: -860

Chapter 22 – Olympus Mons:
    On Gameknight999 Minecraft Server

AVAILABLE NOW FROM MARK CHEVERTON AND SKY PONY PRESS

THE GAMEKNIGHT999 SERIES
The world of Minecraft comes to life in this thrilling adventure!

Gameknight999 loved Minecraft, and above all else, he loved to grief—to intentionally ruin the gaming experience for other users.

But when one of his father's inventions teleports him into the game, Gameknight is forced to live out a real-life adventure inside a digital world. What will happen if he's killed? Will he respawn? Die in real life? Stuck in the game, Gameknight discovers Minecraft's best-kept secret, something not even the game's programmers realize: the creatures within the game are alive! He will have to stay one step ahead of the sharp claws of zombies and pointed fangs of spiders, but he'll also have to learn to make friends and work as a team if he has any chance of surviving the Minecraft war his arrival has started.

With deadly Endermen, ghasts, and dragons, this action-packed trilogy introduces the heroic Gameknight999 and has proven to be a runaway publishing smash, showing that the Gameknight999 series is the perfect companion for Minecraft fans of all ages.

Invasion of the Overworld (Book One):
$9.99 paperback • 978-1-63220-711-1

Battle for the Nether (Book Two):
$9.99 paperback • 978-1-63220-712-8

Confronting the Dragon (Book Three):
$9.99 paperback • 978-1-63450-046-3

AVAILABLE NOW FROM MARK CHEVERTON AND SKY PONY PRESS

HEROBRINE'S REVENGE SERIES
From beyond the digital grave, Herobrine has crafted some evil games for Gameknight999 to play!

Gameknight999, a former Minecraft griefer, got a big dose of virtual reality when his father's invention teleported him into the game. Living out a dangerous adventure inside a digital world, he trekked all over Minecraft, with the help of some villager friends, in order to finally defeat a terrible virus, Herobrine, who was trying escape into the real world.

Gameknight thought that Herobrine was gone for good. But as one last precaution before his death, the heinous villain laid traps for the User-that-is-not-a-user that would threaten all of the Overworld, even if the virus was no longer alive. Now Gameknight is racing the clock, trying to stop Herobrine from having one last diabolical laugh.

The Phantom Virus (Book One):
$9.99 paperback • 978-1-5107-0683-5

Overworld in Flames (Book Two):
$9.99 paperback • 978-1-5107-0681-1

System Overload (Book Three):
$9.99 paperback • 978-1-5107-0682-8

EXCERPT FROM TERRORS OF THE FOREST

A BRAND NEW GAMEKNIGHT999 ADVENTURE

They left the mushroom biome behind and moved into a snowy forest. The air was cold and biting, freezing Gameknight's nose and cheeks. His breath puffed out before him like smoke that instantly disappeared as it left his mouth. This reminded him of the wintery biomes in the Overworld, but there was something still unusual about it. Far to the left, he could see something that looked like a massive, translucent wall. It was almost as if it were made of blue glass . . . strange.

The atrocity at the mushroom castle weighed heavily on Gameknight's mind. He was confident it was meant to be a message from Entity303; that user was demonstrating his willingness to destroy anything to achieve his goal. Now they understood each other perfectly.

Crafter was furious. He couldn't believe anyone could be so ruthless. Hunter and Stitcher were both anxious to exact some revenge, though Stitcher talked about it as if this were some kind of game. Woodcutter and Herder formed theories why the crazed user would do something so terrible, trying to come up with some justification that would explain this insane behavior. Digger and Empech remained silent, the shock of what they'd seen was still etched deep into the scowls they wore on their square faces.

Fletcher seemed the angriest, though also the quietest. He was boiling with anger, his eyes almost glowing with rage, but he was keeping it all bottled up. The large villager hadn't spoken a word since leaving the mushroom biome, but his body was tense like a coiled spring, ready to explode in some unknown direction. Gameknight felt he needed to get the large villager to talk.

"Fletcher, tell me of your family," Gameknight asked.

The villager seemed shocked by the question. An uneasy silence fell across the group, only the crunch of their boots on the freshly fallen snow making any sound.

"You know what happened to my family." Fletcher adjusted his iron armor, his large shoulders and round belly fitting poorly under the chest plate and leggings. "After all, you were there."

"I don't remember, sorry," the User-that-is-not-a-user said. "I didn't live through that timeline. In my past, Weaver was an important person and things progressed differently for me than they did for you. Can you tell me what happened?"

"Well, Herobrine was in dragon form," Fletcher explained. "I don't know if you remember that?"

Gameknight nodded. "Yes, he did that in my timeline as well."

"When he finally attacked and turned everything into End stone, some of the spiders attacked just ahead of the transformation wave. Those fuzzy beasts . . ." Fletcher grew silent as the nightmare replayed itself through his memory. He moved away from the rest of the group and walked by himself, hiding his tears from the others.

"Great . . . now look what you've done," Stitcher said with a frown.

"What did I do?" Gameknight asked softly. "What happened?"

Crafter moved to his side and spoke softly.

"His family was caught in the spiders' webs," the young NPC explained. "They were caught by the transformation wave. Fletcher had to watch from the safety of an obsidian platform while his family was changed from flesh and blood to pale End stone."

Crafter grew quiet as he, too, relived the terrible moments. The birds and animals in the forest seemed to feel the solemn nature of the moment and grew quiet as well. The only thing audible was Fletcher's sobs. Gameknight didn't know what to say.

When there were no more tears left to be shed, Fletcher returned and finally broke the silence. "If we had been able to destroy more of the monsters before Herobrine arrived, maybe those spiders wouldn't have been there." The big NPC sighed.

"When we fought that battle, we used minecarts with TNT in them, and hidden TNT cannons to blast the monsters," Gameknight said.

"What do you mean? Minecarts with TNT? Cannons?" Crafter asked.

"Much of it was actually your idea, Crafter," Gameknight said. "You were the TNT master . . . in my timeline."

"I wish we'd had that in our battle," Fletcher said.

"They were restored when the dragon was killed, weren't they?" Gameknight asked.

Fletcher sighed, then glanced down at the ground with fists clenched. A lone tear trickled down his flat cheek.

"Gameknight, Herobrine destroyed everyone that was transformed," Crafter said. "Even though they were no longer a threat, Herobrine flew around and shredded them with his dragon claws, regardless if they were warriors, women, children, the elderly . . . he destroyed them all."

"You mean your wife and daughter . . ." Gameknight's voice trailed off as the sorrow of what he just asked Fletcher to relive hit him hard in the chest. "Fletcher, I'm so sorry. I didn't know."

Fletcher sighed as more tears tumbled down his cheeks.

"But we ended up destroying that dragon in the end," Stitcher said in a loud, triumphant voice. The volume of her comment was shocking, shattering the uneasy silence.

"But too late," Fletcher moaned.

The User-that-is-not-a-user placed a hand on the large NPC's shoulder. Fletcher turned and looked straight into his eyes and moved a little closer. He reached into his inventory and pulled out a shattered piece of End stone wrapped in a soft, red cloth.

"This is a piece of my daughter," the large villager said, his red eyes filled with despair. He then leaned in close and spoke in a quiet voice, his words only meant for Gameknight's ears. "If getting Weaver back into your past will save my family, then I'll do anything, even sacrifice my own life."

"No one will sacrifice their life," Gameknight whispered. "We're all gonna survive whatever Entity303 has in store for us. We'll stop that crazy user and fix all the damage he's done to Minecraft."

"I hope so," Fletcher said as he wiped his cheeks clean.

One of the wolves far ahead howled. It was the forward scout.

"They found something," Herder said with a smile.

"Come on, let's see what it is," Stitcher said. She sprinted forward, leaping up and down like a child excited for a surprise.

The rest of the party ran toward the howling animals, now more of the proud voices had joined the animal's song. When he sprinted around a cluster of trees, Gameknight saw a huge stone enclosure, the walls decorated with the undulating shape of some kind of serpent. Bright fireflies sat on the side of the wall, their fat bodies glowing bright green, casting some light on the surroundings.

Near the wall sat an oak tree. Gameknight pulled out a shovel and quickly dug up some dirt blocks, then built a set of steps. He climbed to the top of the tree and peered down into the courtyard. The snow, for some reason, did not fall in the enclosure, making things on the ground easy to see. There were numerous creatures moving about; a small herd of deer munched on grass while a singular of boars moved about in the courtyard, doing whatever boars do.

"Weaver's scent went into that enclosure," a voice said at his side. Gameknight turned and found Herder standing next to him. "We need to go in there and see where they came out. Or maybe they didn't come out, and there's a tunnel or cave in there."

Gameknight scanned his surroundings. The ground in the enclosure was covered with grass, stone slabs sprinkled throughout. Maybe twenty columns of stone stood tall throughout the court-yard, with a wide platform of stone slabs at the top and bottom. They were probably six blocks high and a good place to put some archers, just in case.

"Why do you think these walls are here?" Crafter asked from the ground.

"I don't know," Gameknight replied.

"I'm not thrilled with the picture of a serpent on the walls," Hunter said as she drew an arrow from her inventory and notched it to the bowstring.

Stitcher paced about next to her, the younger sister clearly anxious to get in there and see what would happen.

"Empech recommends caution, yes, yes," the little pech said from the ground. "It is not clear if this wall was meant to keep intruders *out*, or something else *in*."

"Weaver went in there," Gameknight said. "I think we need to do the same."

"Excellent," Stitcher said.

"Something ancient lies within these walls, yes, yes," Empech said. "Empech can feel it through the fabric of Minecraft; something angry and dangerous."

"Probably just a spider," Stitcher said. "Let's get started. Weaver's getting farther away as we stand here."

"I hate to say it, but my noisy little sister is right," Hunter added. "We have no choice. If we're gonna catch Weaver, then we need to follow his trail."

"Okay, everyone, up onto the wall," Gameknight said.

He stepped from the tree to the top of the wall, then moved further from the leafy blocks to make room for the others. When everyone was on the wall, he glanced to his friends, then nodded his head. They all jumped down into the enclosure at the same time. Instantly, a scraping sound filled the air.

"Did you hear that?" Digger asked. "I heard something."

"Me, too," Woodcutter said, his axe held at the ready.

"Move forward," Gameknight said.

The companions walked slowly forward, stepping over stone slabs and around pools of black sand. Suddenly, a hissing sound, like that of a massive balloon leaking air, reached their ears, the scraping sound growing louder and louder.

And then a massive, scaly green snake emerged from the haze. It had a huge head that was as tall as Gameknight, with eyes glowing blood-red and filled with rage. Its mouth yawned open, showing a line of pointy white teeth. It stopped for a moment, staring at the intruders.

"The Naga," Empech said in a high-pitched whisper.

"Maybe it's not hostile?" Digger said in a low, shaking voice.

"It is certainly hostile, yes, yes. Empech can feel its anger. All should stand still and. . . ."

The massive green snake suddenly bellowed an ear-splitting roar and charged straight at them, its body smashing through the stone pillars as if they were made of paper. It seemed to come straight at Gameknight999, as if it had been expecting him. Every nerve in the User-that-is-not-a-user's body told him to run, just run away. He didn't want to fail his friends; he just wanted to disappear, but he knew he couldn't do that.

He glanced around to see if anyone noticed his fear—no, his panic. He was terrified he was going to fail here in front of everyone. But he knew he had to do something; Weaver was counting on him, and he didn't want to fail him again. So instead, he focused on what was important, Weaver and his friends.

The giant green snake seemed to move in slow motion, its thick scales dragging against the ground.

Be strong and have faith, child, a voice said in his head. It seemed as if it came from some memory, the voice vaguely familiar. And, for a moment, it filled him with the faintest flicker of courage.

Gritting his teeth, Gameknight999 drew his iron sword from his inventory with his left hand, his diamond blade with his right, and charged straight at the creature, yelling at the top of his voice.

"FOR WEAVER!"

COMING SOON:
TERRORS OF THE FOREST
THE MYSTERY OF ENTITY303 BOOK ONE